The Other One

COLETTE

The Other One

Translated by Elizabeth Tait

and Roger Senhouse

FARRAR, STRAUS AND GIROUX

NEW YORK

1

"THE eleven o'clock postman brought nothing. If
Farou didn't write last night before going to bed,
it's because he'd had a late rehearsal."

"Do you think so, Fanny?"

"I'm certain. *No Woman about the House* isn't difficult to
produce, but that little Asselin's not at all the right type
for Suzanne."

"She's jolly pretty, all the same," said Jane.

Fanny shrugged her shoulders.

"My poor Jane, what point is there in her being pretty?
The part of Suzanne never called for a pretty woman.
What's wanted is a Cinderella like Dorilys. Didn't you
see the original production?"

"No."

"Of course not, what a fool I am! That was nineteen
nineteen!"

"The play doesn't date," said Jane.

Fanny turned on her an eye half veiled by a band of
black hair.

"But it does, my dear. Like all plays, even Farou's.
It's only Farou himself who doesn't date."

"So much the better for you!" said Jane.

"And, at this present moment, for little Asselin," was
Fanny's conclusion.

She laughed good-humouredly and peeled a juicy
peach.

With a tilt of the chin Jane drew her attention to little

Farou, who was busy picking up grains of sugar by pressing them on to his fingers before licking them off, and showed no sign of having heard.

"You do understand," Fanny Farou went on, "that Asselin has been given the part on tour because, after all, the tour includes Deauville, seaside resorts and casinos? On a Casino Tour, it's no small advantage to have, as Asselin has, cars, lovers, dresses, and a paid publicity agent; everything, in fact, that prevents a summer tour from being a complete fiasco. You do understand that, don't you, Jane, pale little Jane?"

"Yes, I do."

She looked pale and preoccupied, as happened most days of the week. For this she hurriedly apologised.

"I didn't sleep well, and then . . ."

Little Farou raised his blue eyes to her when she was least expecting it, and it was to him she automatically addressed her next words.

". . . and then I think there is a rat in the wainscot . . ."

"And a loose shutter, and an owl in the plane-tree, not to mention the wind whistling *w-h-o-o-o* under the door and the kitchen window going *clickety-clack*," Fanny enumerated. "Well, Jean, have I left any of them out?"

She laughed, and the others joined in.

"Jane, my love, do get it into your head that you're just as entitled to be sleepless as lethargic. It's hot, one must live and let live, and while Farou sweats and swears and curses, it's Asselin who's 'catching' it."

"I do admire . . ." Jane began, but once again she encountered little Farou's blue eyes—less blue in the blaze of noon—and she broke off.

"Little Farou, pass me the red currants, *please*."

He obeyed precipitately, his hand brushing against Jane's beneath the electro-plated wire basket. His fingers recoiled with a convulsive movement akin to a spasm of disgust, and he blushed so violently that Fanny burst out laughing.

"There's still the one at four o'clock," Jane said after a moment's pause.

"The one . . . what, at four o'clock?" Fanny enquired, her mouth juicy with the peach she was eating whole.

"Post."

"Oh!" said Fanny, pushing up her band of hair with one finger, "I'd forgotten all about it. That one hardly ever brings anything from Paris. Do you want a drink, little Farou?"

"Yes. Please."

"Please, who?"

"Please, Mamie."

He blushed because he was fair, and because he found his stepmother a little too blunt. Then he relapsed into one of his youthful daydreams, when his outlandish name Farou fitted him like a wattled hut or a grass skirt. His face became expressionless. With eyebrows lowered and the clear line of his mouth half open, he harboured, behind his habitual stolid appearance, a secret eagerness, a sensitiveness tortured by a word or a laugh. He was sixteen.

The shade of a veranda encouraged them, for the midday meal, to drag the big table cleared of newspapers and pieces of needlework as far as the hall entrance. On evenings when Big Farou returned to the bosom of his family, four places were squeezed round the flaking iron pedestal table, which never left the terrace.

"I've eaten too much," sighed Fanny Farou, the first to rise.

"By way of a change," said Jane.

"That cream cheese! Oh, children!"

Languidly she made her way to the broad divan and stretched herself out on it. When lying down, she looked very pretty: pink and white skin, long black hair, prominent, gentle eyes and full, rounded mouth. The only feature she was proud of was her short nose, silvery white with rounded nostrils.

"Fanny Farou, you're getting fat," said Jane in a threatening tone, as she stood over her.

They exchanged a glance full of mischievous understanding. The one knew herself to be beautiful as she lay with her charming nose tilted upward, revealing the plump chin of a woman passionate and at the same time too easy-going: the other held erect a handsome figure betraying no sign of fleshiness, a head crowned with fair hair—if "fair" can be applied to the colour of fine ash—faintly golden at the nape and silvery at the temples. Impelled by genuine solicitude for Fanny's well-being, Jane bent over and plumped up a linen cushion behind her head and covered over her long lazy arms and bare ankles with stiff tulle net.

"There! And don't move, or the flies will get in under the net. Go to sleep, Fanny, you lazy, incorrigible, greedy creature—but not for more than half an hour!"

"What are you going to do, Jane, in this heat? . . . Where's Jean? Whilst the sun is so high, he shouldn't . . . I'll tell his father . . ."

Overcome by the sudden drowsiness that besets the greedy, Fanny's voice petered out into silence. Jane looked for a moment at the relaxed features, at their shape and southern colouring, before she stole away.

To the more rapid beat of her heart Fanny dreamt a dream, commonplace, incomprehensible. She saw the hall, the terrace, the waterless valley, the familiar inhabitants of the villa; but overhead a purplish stormcloud filled

animals and humans, the very landscape itself, with dis-
quiet. A dream-Jane was standing under the veranda,
gazing enquiringly at the empty path below the terrace,
and she was in tears. Fanny woke with a start and sat up,
pressing both hands upon her overladen stomach. In
front of her, under the veranda, stood a very real Jane,
motionless, idle. Reassured, Fanny wanted to call out to
her; but Jane, letting her head drop, pressed her forehead
against the window, and this slight movement detached
from her eyelashes a tear which trickled down her cheek,
sparkled on the downy edge of her lip, and dropped on
to her bodice, where two fingers plucked it delicately
and crushed it as if it had been a breadcrumb. Fanny lay
back, closed her eyes, and fell asleep again.

"Mamie! The post!"

"What, it can't be four o'clock! How long have I been
asleep? And why didn't Jane . . .? Where is Jane?"

"Here, on the ladder," replied the high-pitched, muted
voice which Big Farou called "the angel voice".

Confused both by sleep and her dream, Fanny looked
up in the air for Jane, as though looking for a bird, and
Jean Farou, surprisingly for him, broke into laughter.

"What are you laughing at, you young owl? Would
you believe it, but at the very moment you woke me I
was dreaming that . . ."

But at last she became aware that a large white letter
was dancing in front of her, held at arm's length by Jean,
and she pounced on it eagerly.

"Off you go, errand-boy! No, after all, stay, my
little Jean; it's a letter from our Farou to all of us,
children!"

She read with one eye, the other covered by a riband of
black hair. Her white dress had rucked up and was
wrinkled tight across her chest, and she allowed all and

sundry to gaze upon the vaguely untidy but guileless beauty that gave her a slight look of a creole, or as Farou said "a touch of George Sand". She raised her hand to command attention.

"*Judging by the rehearsals of yesterday and the day before,*" she read, "*I have every reason to believe that the touring company will be excellent, and* No Woman about the House *better acted than it was originally. Little Asselin*—Hi there, Jane!—*Little Asselin is surprising everyone, self included. We are working like angels. We're through with our rows, hysterics, fainting fits, and all that nonsense—and high time too. Oh, my poor Fanny, if women only knew what bores a man can find them when he has no desire to be the cause either of their tears or their happiness!*"

Fanny pushed back her lock of hair with one finger and pulled a comically scandalised face.

"Oh, I say, Jane, I say (Jean, clear off!), it looks to me very much as if poor Farou has, if I dare say so, sacrificed himself."

"It looks to me remarkably like it," Jane repeated after her.

She sat down on the divan beside her friend and with a gentle hand smoothed Fanny's hair and straightened the fine, bluish parting above the left eyebrow.

"What a mess you're in . . . your skirt's all scrumpled up. . . . I'm tired of that frock. Tomorrow I'll go into the town and bring you back a nice length of yellow or pale blue material, and by the time Farou gets back on Saturday, you'll have a new frock."

"Will you?" said Fanny, in an indifferent tone. "Will that be any help?"

They looked at one another, the prominent dark eyes with their thick lashes questioning the grey eyes of the fair-haired friend. Jane shook her head.

"Oh, I do admire you, Fanny. You really are exceptional."

"I? If so, the news would have spread."

"Yes, exceptional. You accept without demur, without resentment, and even without a hint of your own importance, that Farou has . . . sacrificed himself."

"Needs must," said Fanny. "And if I didn't accept it, what difference would it make? None at all."

"Yes, yes, but all the same I confess—yes—I confess . . ."

"That in my place you'd be finding things far from rosy?"

"That's not what I meant," said Jane, evading the issue.

She got up and went out on to the terrace to make sure that little Farou, who could vanish like a snowflake on a warm window pane, was not within earshot.

"Merely this, Fanny, I think that a man who belonged to me, and made me his wife . . . To learn that at this very moment that man is mucking about with some stage tart or other, and to conclude philosophically that 'he has sacrificed himself', that 'the job requires it', well, no, I admire you, but I could never do it!"

"Quite so, Jane. Fortunately no one is asking you to do it."

In a flash Jane was beside Fanny again, curled up at her feet.

"Fanny, you're not vexed with me, are you? There are days when I'm no good to anyone; I'm clumsy, bad tempered, unhappy. You know me so well, Fanny."

She rubbed her cheeks and little round ears against the white frock, feeling with her forehead for her friend's hand.

"You have such lovely hair, my little Jane," Fanny murmured.

Jane gave an affected laugh.

"You say that as if it might serve as an excuse!"

"Up to a point, Jane, up to a point. I can't be cross with a Jane who has such lovely hair. I can't scold Jean when his eyes are so very blue. As for you, you're sprinkled all over, hair, skin and eyes, with a fine silvery ash, with moon-dust, with . . ."

Jane looked up at her with a face suffused with annoyance and sudden tears, and exclaimed, "There is nothing lovely about me. I'm worthless! I deserve to be loathed, cropped, thrashed!"

She let her head fall back into Fanny's lap once more and broke into raucous sobs, whilst the first low rumblings of a thunderstorm faintly reverberated from peak to peak through the echoing foot hills.

"This is her crisis," thought Fanny tolerantly. "It's the thundery weather."

Already Jane was growing calm again, shrugging her shoulders to make fun of herself and discreetly blowing her nose.

'Yet,' Fanny noted, 'she said "stage tart" and "mucking about with". I've never before heard her use slang or vulgar expressions. Coming from her lips, extreme language is tantamount to physical violence. Physical violence in this weather! It's too much of a good thing.'

"What shall we do till dinner-time?"

Jane, still in her suppliant attitude at Fanny's feet, raised her head. "You wouldn't like to go into the town and have tea at the confectioner's? We could walk back."

"Oh!" Fanny's expression was one of horror.

"No? You're putting on weight, Fanny."

"I always put on weight when it's hot and I've more

than ten thousand francs in the bank. You know enough of our 'method of procedure' to realise that I don't often lack opportunities for losing weight."

"That's true. Would you like me to wash your hair? No, you wouldn't? Shall we squeeze the red and black currants left over from lunch? A handful of sugar, a drop or two of Kirsch, pour the juice over the sponge cake we had the day before yesterday and let it soak in thoroughly. We'll serve a little jug of fresh cream separately, and so have an entirely new sweet for tonight, with no cost at all."

"Rather boarding-house," said Fanny with distaste. "I don't care for resuscitated sweets."

"Just as you like, Fanny dear. May the Lord continue to preserve you from boarding-houses, where I certainly learned to use up all sorts of things."

The gentle tone of reproof seemed to tire Fanny who, putting a hand on Jane's shoulder, pulled herself to her feet.

"After all," she exclaimed, "fresh cream, currant juice . . . yes, that will do nicely! On one condition, Jane."

"I mistrust you."

"That you'll attend to this culinary treat yourself. Meanwhile I shall write a line to Farou. I'm going up-stairs to splash myself with cold water, and . . ."

"And?"

"And that's all. It's more than enough!"

When on her feet, she appeared to be smaller than when lying down. She was utterly without any sort of protective coquetry and rolled her fine hips with a slightly vulgar assurance. Jane followed her with her eyes.

"Fanny, when will you make up your mind to wear a girdle?"

"It's a question of temperature, my dear. At five degrees above freezing point, I put on a girdle. You've only to look at the thermometer. And see that the fresh cream doesn't turn sour before this evening. I'm so fond of it."

Jane had made up on her, and started to pull down the hem of her skirt, after deftly pinning up a strand of her long black hair.

"Off you go, you naughty Fanny, all will be well for this evening. I'll even try to get Jean in for dinner by banging a bowl as they do on farms before feeding corn to the hens. What a life you lead your friend!"

She gave a contented laugh and set about collecting faded petals off the table-cloth in the hollow of her hand, blowing away the crumbs, and emptying an ash-tray.

'My friend? . . . Yes, she is my friend. All the same, to say my friend is to say a good deal . . .' Fanny meditated as she made her way slowly up the stairs. 'Who else has ever shown me so much friendship? No one. So she is my friend, a real friend. It's queer that in my own mind I never call Jane my friend.'

No sooner was she alone in the room with its twin beds than she threw off her clothes. The topmost branches of the trees reached as high as the balcony and at night scratched against the closed shutters. For the last two years the neglectful landlord had omitted to have them clipped and the large open bay in the foliage was closing up again little by little. Well wooded and gently undulating, the whole place was imbued with the melancholy atmosphere of a waterless countryside. No river, the sea a hundred leagues away, not a lake to redouble the expanse of the sky. By two o'clock the face of the house and its terrace, in full sun throughout the morning, had resumed their true appearance, criss-crossed with little beams, jutting eaves, and chocolate-coloured shutters, and bathed in an unnatural light, a dreary imitation of the sunlight that reverberated from the hillside opposite. Fanny, barely covered by her chemise, leaned over the balcony and gazed at a landscape which, on leaving it the previous summer, she had expected never to see again.

'It was Farou's idea,' she mused. 'Two summers running in the same district, that's something we haven't often experienced. However, since Farou likes the place . . .'

She turned round and took stock of the room behind her, as big as a barn, and looking larger still with the shadow caused by the half-closed shutters.

'Everything is too big here. With only two servants, how can one be expected to . . . ? If it weren't for Jane, I couldn't stand it.'

Her ear caught the sound of brisk footsteps passing through the hall below.

'She's astounding. In this heat! And so kind, except for her attacks of touchiness. A shade too useful for a friend. That's it, a shade too useful.'

She caught sight in a mirror of her own happy-go-lucky reflection, hands on hips, her dark hair all anyhow, and scolded it. 'What a sight! And I talk about Jane being too useful for a friend! I who can't even tap out Farou's manuscripts!'

She plunged into the cold water as if it were a demonstration of domestic activity, did her hair, put on a last-summer's frock, blue with mauve flowers, and sat down to write. She unearthed a sheet of white paper and a yellow manilla envelope, made do with them, and began her letter to Farou.

"*Dear Big Farou,*

"*Leaving the task of bringing some excitement into your life to one or two little Asselins, I can sum up our existence in a couple of words: no news. We await you. Our busy Jane is devising some choice new dishes; little Farou still looks like a prisoner languishing in the most awkward of all ages; finally, your lazy Fanny . . ."*

A little English song drifted up from the terrace.

'Ah,' thought Fanny, 'it's one of the days when Jane is thinking regretfully of Davidson.'

She was ashamed of herself for her mockery, then wallowed in her shame.

'After all, there's nothing unkind in what I was thinking. On the days when Jane remembers Davidson, she sings in English. On Meyrowicz days she calls out to Jean Farou, "Jean, come here, and I'll teach you a Polish folk-dance!" And when it's Quéméré, she digs up horsy memories, an old, melancholy wistfulness for a certain Breton mare, a roan, very saddle-backed.'

She powdered her face again and watched, on the face of the nearest hillside, the encroaching shadow of another hill.

'This place is depressing. What attraction has it for Farou? To come back two successive summers to the same district, I've never known that to happen before in twelve years of married life. But till now I hadn't noticed how dreary it was here. Next summer . . .'

But her courage failed her at the prospect of twelve months ahead.

'We'll first have to see whether Farou finishes his play and whether he can make something out of a second season at the Vaudeville. But if they revive *Atalanta* at the *Théâtre Français* in October . . . Oh, well, let's forget it: that's real wisdom.'

It was the only wisdom she had learned.

'The most urgent thing is that Farou should come

back here, to work on his third act. We're all so stupid
when he's not here.'

A silent puff of wind stirred the lime branches nearest
the balcony, revealing the white undersides of the leaves.
Fanny finished her letter and went to lean over her balcony, hair loose, shoulders bare. Below her, with arms
crossed on the low wall of the terrace, Jane too was
leaning out over the Franche Comté landscape, so totally
lacking in river, pond, laughter of water, upsidedown
reflections, mists, and the smell of spongy marsh-
flowered river-beds. From far above, Fanny sent a
melodious call winging down to the round head with its
short well-kept hair, ash-coloured and veined with gold,
and Jane, as cats do, bent back her head without turning
round.

"I bet you've been to sleep again."

"No," said Fanny, "actually not. Would you believe it,
I've taken a dislike to this place."

Jane whirled round, and flattened her back against the
brick wall.

"No, not really? Since when? Have you told Farou?
Could you not . . .?"

"Goodness, Jane, don't run on so! Can't I so much as
express a simple opinion without you twisting and turning and tying yourself up in verbal knots, before you
dash your brains out against that wall?"

She laughed, still leaning out, and unfurled a banner of
black hair, before tossing it back over her shoulder.

"*My long tresses fall to the foot of the tower*," sang Jean
Farou, who was walking up the slope towards the terrace.

"Here comes someone," shouted Fanny, "who already
sings as flat as his father!"

"But he's not got Big Farou's voice," said Jane. "Jean,
just do your imitation of Big Farou when he comes home

and says, 'Oh, all these women! Goodness, what a lot of women I've got in my house.' "

Jean walked on past her without answering and disappeared into the hall. Jane gave a toss of her head towards the first-floor balcony.

"My dear, what a look he gave me! His lordship doesn't like to be teased!"

"Nobody likes being teased at his age," said Fanny thoughtfully. "We spend our time flaying that child alive without meaning to."

Hearing a footfall on the stairs, she called out, "Jean!"

The boy opened the door of her room and stood there, "Mamie?"

He was wearing, with no loss of dignity, almost poverty-stricken summer clothes—frayed tennis shirt, white linen trousers, green about the knees and too short in the leg, a belt, and rope-soled espadrilles which the caretaker's son would have scorned. He waited for Fanny to speak and breathed through half open lips, patiently turning to his stepmother the sun-tanned, clear, expressive and impenetrable face of a sixteen-year-old boy.

"You are in a state! Where have you sprung from?"

He turned his head towards the window to indicate vaguely that he had come from the countryside, the countryside at large, from the violet of its shadows, from the green of its meadows. His blue eyes shone with an almost tumultuous animal life, but they gave away no secret other than their blueness, their intensity. Down below, Jane took up her little English song again and Jean Farou, slamming the door behind him, went to his room.

'What a ninny!' thought Fanny. 'Now he's in love with Jane. All would be fine, if only she were a little nicer to him.'

Dinner reunited the three of them on the terrace. In Farou's absence, Fanny and Jane kept up a flickering sparkle of gaiety and, whether his father were present or not, Jean Farou maintained an intolerant and rarely broken silence.

"It's curious," said Fanny as she looked up at the clear white sky, "how unrewarding the close of day is here. The sun sets for others, over there behind . . ."

"The aspect of the mountains is monotonous," Jane said.

"Maeterlinck," growled Jean.

The two women burst out laughing and little Farou looked daggers at them.

"I've had enough of your forced merriment!" he shouted as he left the table.

Fanny shrugged her shoulders and watched him go.

"He's becoming impossible," Jane said. "How can you allow him, Fanny . . .?"

Fanny gently raised a white hand, "Hush, Jane, you know nothing about it."

"You are really so kind."

She shook her head and that stirred the soft hair on her forehead and above her very small, almost round ears. When she wanted to convince Fanny of anything, she would open her grey eyes, flecked with gold, to their full extent and, by retracting her upper lip, reveal four small short white teeth. But Fanny paid no attention to what she called Jane's "daughterly expression". She did not enjoy smoking, and now put out her cigarette by crushing it under her thumb with hidden animosity.

"No, Jane, don't keep on telling me that I'm so kind. But let me repeat that you don't understand that child in the slightest."

"Do you?"

"Probably I don't, either. All I know is that we often make little Farou unhappy. You especially. For he is, of course, in love with you. And you sometimes treat him with a rather cruel indifference."

"A fine time to start, I must say!"

"Goodness, Jane, how easily shocked you are! You're pretty, my stepson is sixteen. I know perfectly well that Jean would never dare, perhaps would never wish to make you a 'declaration'."

"He'd better not try!"

Jane left the table and stood with her elbows propped on the low terrace wall.

'That's done it,' thought Fanny. 'She's bitten my head off, and now she'll tell me about the education given to adolescents in England. It's definitely Davidson's day.'

But Jane, when she turned round, had the smiling face of a thirty-year-old child.

"Don't you find it maddening, Fanny," she exclaimed, "that for weeks now there hasn't been a single thing within reach which is really cold, or even cool to the touch? Even after midnight the walls are hot, the silver's warm, the flagstones . . ."

"And who's to blame? That wretched Farou. He wishes to finish the play here."

"You should have stood up for yourself, Fanny, stood up for us all, even for the houseboy, who is wilting away!"

She frowned, knitting her ash-pale eyebrows accentuated by a pencilled line, and looked disapprovingly at the landscape which was settling down to rest in the dry evening air.

"But you said 'yes', and 'yes' again. If only your slavish 'yes-my-dear-isms' produced some results. Really, women are . . ."

"Kss . . . Kss . . ." Fanny hissed.

Jane held her tongue, and blushed after her fashion, that is to say her fawn complexion darkened a shade.

"I'm meddling in something which doesn't concern me, I know . . ."

"Oh what does it matter?"

No sooner were the words out of her mouth, than it occurred to Fanny that so ambiguous an absolution could hurt Jane, and she added, "Jane, don't be quite such a tease with little Farou. He's sixteen. It's hard on a boy of that age."

"I've been through that age myself. And no one was sorry for me."

"But you were a girl. That's altogether different. And besides," Fanny said, in response to a pathetic glance, "at that age, or thereabouts, in sheer desperation you ended by tossing a rose to a passer-by, on the other side of the wall."

"That's true, that's true," Jane agreed, suddenly softening. "You're right as usual, Fanny. I tell you, I'm bad, wicked, illogical."

She hugged Fanny's shoulders tight, resting her cheek against the loosely knotted black hair, and repeated "I'm bad, bad . . ."

"But why?" asked Fanny, who rarely bothered with polite lies.

Jane pushed back her head and looked up at the pink sky in all innocence, showing her four little teeth.

"How should I know! I'm not one of life's spoilt darlings. Old resentments have a way of poking up their ugly noses. Dearest Fanny, protect me! Don't tell Farou that I've been so . . . so impossible whilst he's been away."

There they stayed till lamp-time, shoulder against

shoulder, with few words passing, silently pointing to a bat, a star maybe, listening to the faint fresh breeze in the trees, imagining the reddening glow of the sunset they never saw unless they climbed the hill opposite.

Below, on the top terrace, there was a crunch of gravel.

"Hello, Jean Farou!" called out a docile Jane.

"Yes?" a hoarse young voice answered.

"Shall we put on a record? Or play a game of patience?"

"All right. . . . Yes. . . . Just as you like," said the sulky voice.

But he bounded up so quickly that Fanny was startled to see him close beside them, all white except for his face and arms, and illumined by the tragic halo that encircles the head of an adolescent.

Jane slipped her hand under his arm in a sisterly fashion and drew him towards the card-table, whose moth-eaten green cloth smelt of mould and stale cigars.

"Hello, boy!" she said in English.

'Decidedly,' thought Fanny, satisfied, 'it's Davidson's day.'

2

"A RE you listening?"
"I'm listening."
"Is it still the stolen letters scene?"

"I think so. Yesterday morning he gave me fifteen pages to type. Five minutes later he snatched them back, looking as if . . . as if . . ."

"I know," laughed Fanny, "as if you'd taken away the bone he was gnawing. What else can you expect! He can never achieve the throes of creation save to the accompaniment of thunder and lightning. What do you think of the first two acts?"

"Sublime," said Jane.

"Yes," said Fanny thoughtfully. "It's disquieting."

From the house rose a murmur as of a prayer meeting, a congregation at Mass, the initial stages of a riot. When this died down, the solemn responses of the last bees were audible in the air as they worked high among the topmost lime flowers and ivy blossom. The rasping cry of a wild animal interrupted the muttered office being celebrated behind the half-opened shutters; but neither of the two women—nor indeed Jean Farou, sprawled over the wickerwork couch, a book between his idle hands—even so much as turned a hair.

"It's always the same end-scene—Branc-Ursine caught red-handed attempting to force the locked drawer," said Fanny. "Where in the world shall we be able to take refuge when there are two Farous writing and intoning their plays?"

The blue of Jean's eyes, as he looked up, was dazzling.

"I shall never write plays, Mamie, never."

"It's far easier to give up than to try," was Jane's immediate rejoinder.

"Giving up isn't always the easiest way out," said Jean.

He blushed at the boldness of his reply, and Fanny noticed how the mounting blood spread up the boy's open neck to quicken the pulse behind his ear.

"Come, Jane, don't torment your young friend any more."

"I enjoy teasing him, it's true," said Jane good-humouredly. "It suits him so well. I forget exactly which day it was, but he looked charming with a tear poised between his lashes."

A silver thimble glinted on the finger with which she was playfully threatening him. Fanny lifted her forehead with its silky black band.

"What! He too!"

"He too?" Jane repeated. "Explain, Fanny dear, explain yourself!"

She was laughing, sewing, and darting happy glances on all around from her grey, amber-speckled eyes: over her unprotected head played a bright medallion from the last rays of the sun, and she seemed almost joyful on this unrewarding summer evening, redolent of sun-baked granite.

"The other day . . ." Fanny began. "Wait, it was the day Farou's letter came, and none of us knew—he least of all—that he'd be able to get back so soon."

"Wednesday," said Jean without looking up.

"Perhaps. . . . I had dozed off after lunch and on waking I saw you standing beneath the veranda where we are now. There was a teardrop about to fall from your eyelid; it trickled down your cheek, and you plucked it—just like that—between two fingers, as if it had been a small strawberry or a grain of rice."

As she listened, Jane's expression changed from smiles to childish sulkiness, and then to wheedling reproach. With her little cleft chin she pointed to Jean Farou.

"Fanny, Fanny, respect my little secrets, my temperamental moods, in front of a listener so . . . so . . ."

She broke off abruptly and over her face spread a look of stupefaction. Fanny turned her head to see her stepson erect, his mouth open as if to utter a cry. He threw both arms in the air and fled, taking the terrace steps two at a time.

"What's . . . what's the matter with him?"

"I don't know," said Jane. "He threw up his arms, as you saw for yourself, and rushed away."

"He frightened me . . ."

"There's no reason why he should," said Jane.

She removed the thimble from her skilled needle-woman's finger, and carefully picked the snippets of thread from her frock.

"He's behaving as one does at his age," she continued. "An exaggerated romanticism. He'll get over it."

"Do you think so?"

Fanny methodically folded up a width of natural coloured linen, a table-cloth she was decorating with red flowers embroidered with large clumsy stitches. She went out and leaned over the low wall and called, "Jean, are you there?"

A rather mocking voice rose from below, imitating her own, "Wolf, are you at home?"

"Stupid creature!" Fanny shouted. "You'll be hearing more from me! Behaving like a great tragic actor! Get on with you, you third-rate comedian! You great . . ."

She straightened up without finishing her sentence, and pivoted round on her fine hips, which belonged by rights, according to Big Farou, to a happier era. She had just heard her husband's voice close at hand.

"There we are, he's finished!" she said in rapid tones to Jane.

"For today. . . ." Jane said dubiously.

Shor˙ ﹍er against shoulder, they watched Farou making his way towards them. He appeared to be sleep-walking, to be emerging gradually from his day's work, in the course of which, muttering, ruminating, or bellowing his third act at the top of his voice, he had unconsciously removed collar, shantung coat, tie, and waistcoat. Six feet from ground level he held a greying head with curly hair partly tumbling over his forehead, where it merged with eyebrows to shade his yellow eyes. Tall, tired, thick-set, ugly maybe, but ever certain of pleasing, his usual pace was that of a man striding into battle or to the scene of a fire: so much so that, when he went through the village to buy cigarettes, mothers would gather their children to the shelter of their petticoats.

He was nibbling a rose, and stared right through the two women. He was still in the dark and luxurious boudoir where the public prosecutor, Branc-Ursine, was demeaning himself to the extent of breaking open a writing-desk to steal the letters which would ruin beautiful Madame Houcquart, the mistress he no longer loved.

"Handsome Farou!" called Fanny tenderly.

Jane's softer voice mimicked her playfully, "Handsome Farou!"

And so faithful was the imitation that Fanny, surprised, mistook it for an echo.

Farou, struck by the double call and by the arrestingly

heavy scent of a Spanish honeysuckle, stopped in his tracks and intoned his ritual ditty, "Ah, all these women! All these women! What a lot of women I've got in my house!"

He yawned, then seemed to wake up and discover the world about him. He hitched up his shantung trousers which were slipping down, and scratched his head. Trustful by nature and devoid of personal vanity, he was happy most of the time and young, at forty-eight, as are men who will countenance, in the ordinary run of their lives, only the company of women.

"Who called me first?" he cried.

He did not wait for an answer but began to dance, singing in a pleasantly off-key voice an improvised line or two in which he insulted, in plain unvarnished military terms, M. Branc-Ursine, the lovely Mme Houcquart, and all their machinations. But of a sudden he caught sight of his son ascending the steep steps to the terrace, changed his tune and clowned for the benefit of the admiring Fanny and Jane, "Cheese it, the cops!"

"Finished, Farou?"

Fanny contrived to hide the measure of her anxiety. Farou before now had pulled so many third acts out of the mire with a final heave of the shoulder. . . . He was gazing at her with a wild but kindly eye.

"Finished? You do have some bright ideas!"

"Yes, but all the same, you've made some progress?"

"Progress? Yes, of course I've progressed. I've chucked out the whole bally scene."

"Oh!" said Fanny, as if he had broken a vase.

"That's good work, that is, my poppet. Jane, be ready to type the final version!"

He clapped his hands and strode to and fro like an ogre.

"Until today, it was going very badly. But today . . ."

"How, pray, did M. Branc-Ursine behave himself today? Did that rascally lawyer hide the letters in a safe place?"

Fanny, who was busy combing Big Farou's hair, folded up her cheap pocket-comb and stood to one side to avoid the blast of his reply.

"I should very much like it if Jane," said Farou casually, "could add a knowledge of graphology to her already varied and numerous accomplishments."

"But I can certainly learn," cried Jane. "There are text books. I know of an excellent manual. Why?"

"I have been told on good authority that a graphologist becomes immersed in the significance of handwriting, in the crossing of *t*s and the looping of *l*s, and is therefore incapable—in so far as the sense is concerned—of reading the manuscripts entrusted to him or to her."

Jane blushed furiously. "Is that a reproof?"

"Not a serious one."

"But one which I shall hold against you."

Farou's yellow eyes flashed.

"Don't put on your 'jobbing dressmaker's' expression, it doesn't impress me, Jane."

She bit her lip, restrained a couple of tears, and Fanny took up the cudgels with the ease of a woman accustomed to such outbursts.

"Farou, you brute! Aren't you ashamed of yourself? All this for the sake of that blackguard Branc-Ursine! Tell me, Farou, does he still steal the letters from that piece of furniture?"

"And what else should he do?"

She pulled a face and rubbed her charming nose with her finger.

"Aren't you afraid it will be rather . . . cinema, or rather . . . theatrical?"

"Rather theatrical? Whatever next!"

He railed at her, as from a great height, mercilessly.

"Yes, I really mean it," Fanny insisted.

He threw his great arms wide apart.

"Now what would you do yourself if you knew that in the safe, drawer, or what-have-you, were locked some letters from a man who had been the lover of—give your nose a good blow, Jane, and come and give us your advice —what would you do, Fanny?"

"Nothing."

"Nothing," echoed Jane in a similar tone.

"Oh, my poor dears, you say that, but——"

"Nothing," came the decisive voice of Jean Farou who, reassured by the shadows, had returned with the dusk.

"Nit-wit," growled Farou.

"Now that Jean considers that nothing should be done . . . Come here, psychologist, come a little closer. You're looking none too well nowadays."

"It's the heat, Mamie."

"The fact is . . . I know someone who is going to sleep on the little sofa tonight," Big Farou proclaimed, "and that's me."

"No, it's me!" said Fanny.

"And I'm going to sleep on the terrace," chimed in Jane.

"Not me," said Jean.

"Why, Jean?"

"Full moon, Mamie. Cats and young lads go on the prowl at night."

In the deepening dusk his hair, eyes, and luminous teeth gave him a phosphorescent look, and he seemed to quiver like a well-spring. His father looked him over with a brief glance that lacked both charity and paternal pride.

"At your age . . ." he began.

" 'I had already slain and begotten a man'," the youngster quoted.

Farou smiled, flattered.

"What's that! What's that!"

"That's a fine thing," Jane said in reproach.

"It's only a quotation," Farou said with condescension.

The eyes of youth were fixed on Farou in an open stare which, whether in meaningless amazement or charged with secrets, remained unfathomable.

The whistle of the evening train, as it trundled sadly along the track that encircled the nearest hill, shrilled from above the village already enveloped in blue mist. A moon the red of quenched embers left the horizon and rose into the sky.

"Where are you going, Jane?"

"I'm going down to the lower terrace, O Grand Inquisitor, and then I'm coming back, I ate too much for dinner."

"Three spoonfuls of rice and a handful of red currants," said Fanny.

"Makes no difference. Aren't you coming down too, Fanny?"

"To climb all that way up again!" Fanny was horror stricken.

The white dress and the little English song faded away into the distance. Fanny lifted her husband's heavy arm and placed it across her shoulders. He did not resist and his fingers lightly touched her breast. Bending down her head, she imprinted a kiss on his hand, a slightly hairy hand, the texture of a sage leaf, the wrist lighter in colour, softer, and green veined. Defenceless and trusting, the hand submitted to this almost timid caress.

"How sweet you are," said Farou's dreamy voice above her head.

The timid mouth pressed more firmly on his wrist and manly hand, shaped for plough or hoe, or to bear arms, but never wielding anything heavier than a fountain pen. He stood with his eyes open, seemingly asleep, resting on his wife's shoulder.

'Perhaps he's already asleep,' she mused. She dared not break their friendly embrace. She breathed in the healthy smell of warm flesh scented with lotion on the hand and arm abandoned to her care. She did not say to herself, 'This man, who lets me bear the weight of his arm was, is still, my one great love.' But there was not a line of the palm or wrinkle encircling the already ageing wrist that did not evoke some amorous memory and revive her passion for rendering service, her certainty that she belonged to one man and had never belonged to any other.

The stealthy sound of a cat parted the leaves and a slender body slid close to the trunk of a lime tree.

'It's Jean,' thought Fanny. 'He's keeping close watch on Jane below.'

She was about to laugh and draw Farou's attention, when she thought better of it. The shadows cast by the trees directly in front of the moon dappled the gravel with blue, and in a twinkling the sky had become a night sky.

"It would have been less hot in Brittany," Fanny sighed out loud.

Farou withdrew his arm and seemed aware that he was not alone.

"In Brittany! Why in Brittany? Aren't we comfortable here?"

"Oh, you . . . you're nothing but a sand lizard."

"We're not working badly here. Do you want us to leave?"

"Oh, no, not now. I was thinking of next year. We won't be coming back here next year?"

A broad pair of shoulders were raised to denote total ignorance.

"There are a number of inconveniencies here. It gets extremely hot without one having enough sun. The boy's not comfortable in his room, which is really baking. He ought to move out of it."

"Of course he should!"

"You stagger me! You know there's not another room for him."

"Nonsense. There's always another room."

"Yes, the east room."

"Which east room?"

"The room Jane is occupying."

"If Jane is occupying it, then it certainly isn't available."

"But will Jane still be with us next year?"

Farou turned ingenuously towards his wife.

"I really don't know. How should I know? Why think of it?"

"Because of Jean."

"What, is he complaining now?"

"Oh stuff, Farou! It would certainly not be like him to complain. Especially if it were to make things uncomfortable for Jane, don't you see!"

"Oh really?"

Fanny saw Farou's eyebrows meet above his yellow eyes over which a spark of moonlight played. The wind sent a few flower-heads and shrivelled leaves bowling along the ground. A light step sounded on the gravel almost indistinguishable from the sound of the leaves, and Jane's white dress reappeared at the end of the terrace. At the further end Jean landed lightly as he sprang from the main branch of one of the lime trees.

"Children," Farou declared, "I don't know whether you're like me, but I'm dropping with sleep."

"That means that everyone must go to bed," said Jean.

"Precisely. And you, Jane, may return to your east room."

"So I've got an east room, have I?" and she gave a shake of her head to flutter her hair.

"Yes, Moon Dust, east room. Cooler than the others. Fanny's just told me."

"Whatever were you talking about?" asked Jane involuntarily. "Oh, I beg your pardon! What bad manners I've got."

"Sometimes," Farou conceded. "Give us your paw. Good night, Jane. Lead the way, son!"

"Oh, Daddy, at a quarter to ten! In this weather! If it isn't a shame!"

A drooping houseboy was dragging himself round the villa, switching on here and there the low-powered, reddish electric light. Farou went straight on through the hall, gave a lion-like yawn at the foot of the stairs, and absent-mindedly shook his son's hand. Once behind the closed door of his sweltering room, Jean Farou began to follow Jane's every movement, as revealed by the creaking floorboards.

3

Fanny Farou's life in Paris had flowed on more or less peacefully, despite the comings and goings of creditors, actors, draughts, and flitting servants. She carried her own peace about with her, together with that indispensable *vade mecum* of the chilly, a plaid, in her case a soft vicuna wrap, the long hairs of which collected cake crumbs. Farou's gesticulating shadow had first fallen on her during a rehearsal of *No Woman about the House*, when she was playing the piano off-stage during the Evening Party act.

"You look like a half-husked hazel-nut, between your bands of black hair," Farou had fired at her as early as their first encounter. Never one to dress well, on that occasion a broken sock-suspender trailed over one of his shoes.

"You're as white-skinned as a half-caste, come with me," he had commanded her ten days later.

"But . . . what will my parents . . .? I am . . . I'm a respectable girl," protested a horrified Fanny.

He looked indescribably bored. "Oh, what a nuisance! Since it can't be helped, we'll get married, if that's what you want!"

In Paris the Farous—three of them, counting young Jean, now legitimised—had lived on next to nothing. Then Farou's plays, rather heavily loaded with purple passages and acts of brutality he thought perfectly natural, moved down from Les Batignolles to the fashionable theatres on the boulevards, where they developed the habit of running for more than a hundred performances. The personality and character of Farou-the-Recluse were called into service for Farou-the-Author. Porto-Riche dubbed him "vulgar", for the simple reason that he was vulgar when with Porto-Riche. He refused point-blank— in barrack-room terms and as a humiliating fatigue-duty— to collaborate with a member of the Académie Française. Bataille wrote patronisingly of his "crude if disarming, easy-going absurdities"; Farou was like a certain three-act play, *The Bargee*, by Flers and Caillavet, for he took a delight in posing as a tramp or a foundling in the presence of those who did not know that for many years Old Pa Farou had taught history to twelve-year-old boys at an obscure public school.

Once they had attained notoriety, the Farous lived like princes, without ever giving it a second thought. Like princes, they lived in a glass house, thanks to reporters, gossip writers, stage fans and fellow actors; but nothing is more opaque than a shimmering glass house. After the fashion of a reigning monarch, Farou was credited with brilliant and short-lived love affairs, yet such trifling incidents in no way diminished Fanny's attractions for him. In between runs they got into debt like princes, but, in a princely fashion, continued to enjoy humble pleasures. Farou would expatiate on the excellence of a homely dish of piping hot food, and often rated idleness at its proper worth. Behind locked doors, he would sit in his shirt sleeves browsing over magazines, while Fanny, one shoe on and one shoe off, her long hair streaming down either cheek, inclined her gentle gazelle-like face over a pack of cards and would re-start a game of patience a score of times.

A young companion shared their bliss. From early childhood, Jean Farou had pressed his baby forehead, as later his boyish chin, against Fanny's elbow to give his stepmother the benefit of his advice, "You've missed your chance of a club sequence, Mamie, and you're done for."

The child, who was said to be lovable because he was pretty and gentle because his eyes were so blue, returned Fanny's absent-minded affection and took her side whenever he guessed her to be displeased with Farou, or down in the dumps. The kindliness she showed her stepson was more general than particular, for she loved and cherished in him some mysterious emanation of his father.

"You're quite sure you haven't kept a picture of his mother?" Fanny would ask her husband. "I should so much have liked to see what she really looked like."

Farou replied with a typical gesture—arms flung wide apart—one that sent flying all memories, regrets, and responsibilities.

"Damned if I can lay my hands on one! A pleasant creature, though, none too robust, poor dear."

"Intelligent?"

Farou's wandering golden glance rested on his wife in astonishment. "I knew so little of her, you know."

'That I can well believe,' thought Fanny to herself. 'Will he say the same about me, if ever . . .'

She never risked going beyond that 'if ever'; her conjecture was sheer bravado, since she was incapable of imagining a life without Farou, without his physical presence, his liturgical mutterings, his way of kicking a door shut to punish a recalcitrant third act, his insatiable craving for women, his moments of gentleness when she would whisper tender and primitive words of praise into his ear.

"You are gentle . . . gentle and soft as a sage leaf . . .

smooth as a finger nail. You are as gentle as a resting stag."

She was so surely established as favourite that she was never to cavil over his right, common to all reigning despots, to sow a few bastards.

"Handsome Farou! Unkind Farou! Intolerable Farou!"

In soft undertones, or in her heart, she would name him with no further comment, like a true believer for whom the litany is all sufficing. During the first years of marriage she had tried to serve her master by day as well as by night; but Farou impatiently discouraged her zeal as an untrained secretary. Restricted to her duties as a paramour, she soon became a fatalist inclined to child-ishness, greed, and self-indulgence, as lazy as those women who, labouring under the weight of a great passion, find themselves tired out by the middle of the day.

Once when seated at the back of the box at the *Théâtre Français*, as the dress rehearsal of *Atalanta* was coming to an end and in reply to Farou's triumphant "Well?" Fanny had taken it upon herself to say, "The scene be-tween Piérat and Clara Cellerier is definitely too long. If you were to bring someone on in the middle with coffee or a telegram, the scene would pick up again much better afterwards, and it would give the audience a break." Since that time, Farou had never again asked for her opinion which, none the less, she never failed to express. If, peevish under criticism, he shot a "Whatever next!" at his wife, reinforced by a glance as weighty and yellow as gold, Fanny would thereupon display a strange freedom of mind and speech. She would expound her views, become insistent even, raising her broad eye-brows with a detached and casual air.

"Of course, as far as I personally am concerned, I

don't mind either way; do as you please. But you'll never make me, as a member of the audience, think it natural that a woman should wish to kill herself for so slight a reason."

"So slight a reason!" exclaimed Farou. "A woman betrayed in such a cold, calculated manner! So slight a reason! Really!"

Fanny tilted her nose and through half-closed lids gave Farou a look of unwonted impertinence.

"Perhaps it isn't so unimportant. But do you want me to tell you what your Denise's behaviour amounts to? It's a man's reaction, and nothing else. A man's re-action!"

Whatever she did, he refused to re-enter the discussion, sometimes exercising a tact vouchsafed only on such occasions. More often, he would break off the conversation with a sudden cry or exclamation.

"My collar stud, good God! And Coolus' letter? Where is that letter from Coolus? In the suit I wore yesterday? Does nobody ever empty my pockets for me? Do they?"

As she ran hither and thither, losing a bedroom slipper, scattering the tortoiseshell prongs that kept her long, unfashionable hair in place, Fanny's colour, expression and language would change; twelve years of matrimonial life had never cured her of her particular form of rever-ence, in which Farou's talent and fame counted for con-siderably less than he would have been willing to believe. Highly emotional, she was wise enough to accustom herself to the uncertainties of life. With unimaginative patience and the dignity of a faithful employee, she stood between Farou and his creditors. But once "Bloch's advance payment" had been overspent and the royalties on film rights had come to an end, she had no ideas

beyond getting rid of the car, selling her furs, and pawn-
ing her ring.

"It's curious how behind the times you are! By jingo,
you ought to get a better grip on things!" was the advice
of Clara Cellerier, of the *Théâtre Français*.

That great second-rate actress, well known to all yet
with never a hope of becoming famous, pityingly shook
her beautifully trimmed, green-gold hair, tightly fitted into
a small hat. Daringly dressed, her slender figure sheathed
in youthful black, Clara Cellerier betrayed her sixty-
eight years in nothing except her use of the expression "By jingo!", by a certain military tomboyishness
and her tendency to describe a man as a "dashing
horseman".

"She never mentions a man who's been known to go
on foot," Berthe Bovy declared.

Clara treated Fanny as a young country cousin, with
the warmheartedness of a "good trouper", with a "Cheer
up, child!", with beauty recipes and addresses of "clever
little seamstresses round the corner". But Fanny, in her
heedlessness, never bothered about her clothes and wore
the same gowns two years running, although she was
sometimes to be seen in furs. She had the otter-fur from
Atalanta, the mink from *No Woman about the House*,
and from *Stolen Grapes* the blue foxes, which she sold
when *The Swap* was a resounding flop to teach Farou a
lesson for giving a wartime setting to the story of a pair
of lovers who had no idea there was a war on.

Fanny was never to forget that difficult turning-point:
no money, or next to none, little Farou down with
typhoid fever, and the maid taking to her heels for fear of
infection. That was the moment chosen by the police to
nab the Farous' manservant, in their own pantry, on a
charge of indecent behaviour. Farou himself, withdrawn

from the world while in the throes of the fourth act of his
new play and hammering with his fists on the table and
doors, bemoaned the fact that his shorthand-typist, Mme
Delvaille, had allowed herself to be brought to bed before
his fourth act had seen the light of day.

"It never rains but it pours," he shouted from afar,
behind closed doors.

"How right you are," Fanny sobbed quietly as she
squeezed lemons for feverish little Farou, her hair lustre-
less over her faded bed-jacket.

One morning under hospital lighting, amid layers of
dust, curling carpet edges, lemon rinds, stray bedroom
slippers, the smell of a badly regulated geyser, eau-de-
Cologne and cold compresses, Fanny awoke on the divan
bed from which she had been dragged during the night
by husky calls of "Mamie, I'm hot . . . Mamie, something
to drink", and felt surging within her an irritation akin
to that of an animal at the end of its tether or of a woman
with a pretty, rather weak chin.

'I've just about had enough. The charwoman's late.
We haven't the money to pay for a nurse. Farou considers
it all quite natural and thinks only of his third act. . . .
I'm going to wake him up, that I am, and give him a piece
of my mind, and hand him back his brat, that I will, and
show him that it's jolly well his turn to . . .'

But little Farou moaned the name Mamie, and Fanny
listened, as if for the first time, to this child who even
when delirious looked for help to none other than to the
woman who was not his mother. She went back to heating water, rinsing basins, squeezing oranges, and grinding coffee beans.

That same morning a charming young woman rang
the doorbell, asked for "The Master", and informed him
that Mme Delvaille had been "successfully brought to

bed of a fine eight-pound boy" and could scarcely resume her duties for another three months. She offered her temporary services to a fierce, silent Farou, who nodded his acceptance. During the days following, Mlle Jane Aubaret, with a comforting show of good humour, lunched with the Farous on a corner of the table, remade the sick boy's bed and doped Fanny with egg yolk beaten up in port. Little by little Jane gave evidence of her capabilities. Helped by Fanny, who was beginning to take heart again, the pair of them got through the work of four servants, each watching the other out of the corner of her eye. By their similar methods of polishing brown shoes, cleaning out the bath without using an abrasive, breaking eggs into a bowl, and lighting the stove without dirtying their hands, each recognised the other as a qualified woman about the house, in the direct line of true middle-class French housewives—those exacting workers who never give a thought to the trouble they take or to their traditional capacity for hard work. In this poor, proud, over-scrupulous bourgeois world, girls are still taught that before going to school mattresses must be turned and beds made, bicycles polished, cotton stockings and gloves washed out in the hand-basin.

Such a collaboration bore fruit. A young, stage-struck manservant replaced the satyr. The housemaid returned. A fresh, tart incense permeated the flat, created by the smell of English apple-pie and furniture polish, and little Farou's temperature went down to normal. Carried along with the rest, Big Farou laughed at dark Fanny and fair Jane, at his son, thin and transparent as a shell, heaved his third act out of the mire, snapped up the Vaudeville under Pierre Wolf's nose, collected a "handsome advance" from Bloch, and amorously tousled his wife.

"Fanny, if there's one piece of advice I have to give you, it's to go at once and choose yourself a fur. Don't put it off too long, Fanny."

She looked at him caressingly, with love-light in her eyes, rubbed her lips and soft velvety nose against his cheek, and her cup was full; she had, unwisely, paid the doctor's bill.

Later Farou said, "And don't forget the present for Jane, since we no longer need her. A wrist-watch, of course."

But neither Farou nor Fanny could have foreseen that when the moment came to say goodbye, Jane would fall into their arms weeping and muttering confused prayers wherein they could detect genuine grief, regrets at leaving "The Master", fear of a dangerous loneliness, the need to devote herself to a friend such as Fanny. . . . Fanny dissolved into tears, Farou's yellow, cat's eyes glistened and Jane promptly explained that a modest income freed her from the least pleasant alternative—to live on her new friends or to accept a salary from them.

The idea of a disinterested friendship is just as intoxicating to middle-class Bohemians as to any other Bohemians. When by themselves the Farous sang Jane's praises and their own pleasure in discovering, in inventing her.

"That girl is perfect," Farou would say, "really perfect!"

"I don't know about her being 'perfect'," Fanny retorted, "but she's certainly worth more than the compliments you make sound like 'references'. You wouldn't believe it, but it was she who cut out and made that *lamé* tunic, so that I could wear out my black marocain pleated skirt."

"Nice way of re-establishing the good name that I have degraded—to use her as a daily sewing woman!

For the matter of that," Farou added, with a look over-flowing with leonine gentleness, "Jane is rather like one of those refined persons who go out to sew for the rich because they cannot abide contact with the poor."

Fanny could not help laughing.

"Heaven preserve me from the 'nice' things you might say about me, Farou!"

In the process of losing her attractions as a newly dis-covered relative, a "nurse" not previously encountered, a novelty friend, Jane shed none of her virtues. She put up with Farou's moods, with his leg-pulling so often more hurtful than his rages, typed rapidly, did all his telephoning. She remembered the telephone numbers of theatres, the names of company secretaries, and knew how to flatter "the good ladies" of the box office. She called Quinson "my great friend", and shared, with no outward sign of astonishment, the financial ups and down of a couple who, trained to do without essentials, strin-gently demanded only the very best.

Blonde Jane—if the colour of the finest wood-ash, that of the poplar, can be called blonde—given her place in the Farous' box, was there accorded her due in the matter of personal sanction by the scandal-mongering members of the audience said to be in-the-know.

"Whose bed does that pretty ash-blonde share? Dark Fanny's, wouldn't you think?"

"No, no, old boy, Farou's of course, the old goat-foot! He invests her with the title of secretary and foists her on his wife."

In reply to a blunt question from Clara Cellerier, Farou settled the matter once and for all.

"Don't lose all sense of shame by letting your imagin-ation run riot, my charming friend. I, like you, hold the classics in respect. There's nothing between Jane—who is my natural daughter—and me, but a simple little case of straightforward incest."

"Where is Jane?" Fanny would ask at all hours of the day, so thoroughly accustomed had she become to encountering a cheerful young woman wherever her eyes might roam.

Jane's ubiquitous presence could have passed for Fanny's one luxury. Her seven years' seniority permitted Fanny a certain ease and freedom in her behaviour and Jane the privileged attentions of a lady-in-waiting or a devoted niece. When Farou returned home he no more thought of greeting Jane than he would a piece of furniture; but her absence brought him up short, "Where's Jane?"

"In her room, I suppose," Fanny would reply. "She's just back from Pérugia's."

"So she buys her shoes at Pérugia's now! My word!"

"And why shouldn't she buy her shoes at Pérugia's if she wants to? As her foot is slightly smaller than mine, and I haven't much go in me today, she took along a woollen stocking and tried on my shoes for me. Do you want me to call her?"

"No, what do you want me to do with her?"

"But you were asking for her a moment ago!"

"Was I? It was for my glass of *vittel-pipérazine*."

"The houseboy's there for that. Soon you'll be making Jane wash your handkerchiefs."

"Well—what about you?"

They exchanged a smile of understanding and reproach.

"Where's Jane?" asked little Farou, tight-lipped and anxious-eyed, brought to a sudden halt as if a taut rope barred him from Jane's empty chair. And Fanny, to pull his leg, often answered him out loud before he had put the question.

In July, the Farous left Paris for a summer resort chosen out of the advertisement columns of *Life in the Country*, or recommended by Clara Cellerier.

Farou felt the need for isolation, for weeks of unorganised work without rules or regulations, and the certainty of not bumping into those whom he called "the ugly mugs". Once away from Paris, it was hard for him to hide his ineptitude for making the most of the lavish gifts of nature—sea, sun, and forest—and Fanny was infected with the uneasiness, the haughty fear of those who have sprung from humble origins.

"There's Pau! They say it's so lovely," was one of Fanny's suggestions. "And you know I've never seen Dinard! Don't you think it funny that at my age I should never have seen Dinard?"

"What I shouldn't think at all funny," growled Farou, "would be to find myself, for instance, having to rub noses with Max Maurey three times a day."

"What's he been up to? Hasn't Max Maurey been treating you well?"

"Of course he has!"

"Well then?"

"That has nothing to do with it, my poppet. You don't understand. It amuses Maurey to change his clothes three times a day during the summer. It doesn't amuse me. Once and for all, I want to spend my summers alone, without shoes and without a stiff collar."

He satisfied his authority as a nomad chieftain by organising the family departures. An ever changing domestic staff followed the Farous, who landed up, equipped with two new trunks and twenty badly tied parcels, at mouldering villas, somberely furnished châteaux, thin-walled cottages, all spots off the beaten track of modern tourists, where Clara Cellerier had once enjoyed clandestine pleasures. Room had to be found for the typewriter, the latest novels, Farou's manuscripts, the dictionary, cabin-trunks and Fanny's plaid, while Jean Farou was put out to grass.

'What will Jane do without us, and we without Jane?' Fanny asked herself in perplexity when July threatened the amicable honeymoon.

But she was reassured when she heard Farou say, "Jane, you'll take *One* and *Two* with you, and all the notes for *Three*. Give the typewriter to the houseboy to bring along by train."

"So that's settled," Fanny sighed.

She faced up cheerfully to the present again and once more settled down amongst french windows, cane armchairs, a new book, the angora wrap, a box of chocolates and the leather cushion. One day, however, she had to allow a past to intrude—Jane's past.

"You really ought to know all about me, Fanny," Jane began.

"Why?" asked Fanny, with whom honesty always took first place over politeness.

"But Fanny, I should die of shame if I kept it back from you. After the way you've taken me into your home! You must know what I am, the bad as well as the good, so that you may judge me."

At this preamble Fanny's eyes, blue-black as those of a thoroughbred mare, began to wander, settling fearfully now on a cloud, now on the lamp, now on a passer-by in the road, anywhere to avoid Jane and her affectionate gaze, Jane and her fluffy hair, Jane and her simple frock, so simple that it was impossible not to notice it.

'Why,' Fanny mused, 'why am I already bored, as I am by the adaptation of an American play? And also why all that formality about pedigrees, branches and collaterals in a home where no one worries about anyone else. Is it really necessary? Is it really decent?'

But Jane was already relating how, as the dowerless child of a Parisian drawing master (You can see some of my father's work at the Duguay-Trouin School, and among it a first-rate charcoal sketch "Donkeys at the Drinking Trough"), she had hurt and bruised and dragged round a tiny garden in Saint-Mandé—between a leafless lilac and laurels in tubs—a haggard, desperate soul, the soul of a young girl who was poor and untrained for any job.

Jane never spoke of these things in front of Farou. She waited until the end of the meal sent him back to his work or his indolence. She waited a little longer, once the two were alone, until Fanny let her book slip from her knees or woke up with an "Anything new, Jane?", refreshed by her siesta. As Jane did not bother to begin at the beginning, Fanny never knew exactly whether Meyrowicz—a most wonderfully handsome Pole and a collectivist, to boot—had taken Jane from Davidson, or whether he had received her from the supple, dangerous hands of the said Davidson, "The" English composer.

'Is there only one composer in England?' Fanny wondered.

She did at least know by heart the story of Antoine de Quéméré, Jane's first misfortune.

"When I used to watch out for my father at the end of the little terrace," Jane would relate, "I used to wait— bent double, like this, over the wall—for such ages before he was due home, that I developed a pain right across my body—here, across the top of my stomach. Eventually, having searched in vain for something new to look at, I became dizzy. I toyed with a flower between my fingers. Girls are little fiends, you know . . ."

'No, I do not know,' was Fanny's unspoken reply.

". . . and on the worst days I would say to myself, 'Suppose a man passes below and I drop my flower. . . .' In the end, I did let go the flower and it fell between the ears of a horse, but on that horse there was a rider!"

'Bravo!' shouted Fanny to herself. 'What a splendid curtain for Act One! What if I put it up to Farou?'

But the next moment she wrinkled her nose.

'Why does it still sound like an English play? Meyrowicz, at least, used to beat Jane. She swears he did, she has also shown me the place on her arm where that disgusting sadist burnt her. These misfortunes of Jane's have about as much effect on me—no, not as much—as *Broken Blossoms* at the cinema.'

"Farou," she said one day to her husband, "can you explain to me why it is that a spinster, when speaking of her former lovers, usually refers to them as her 'misfortunes'? Whereas the self-same gentlemen are called 'Good Fortune No. I', 'Good Fortune No. II' if the good lady is married?"

"Shut up, can't you!" answered the deep, dreamy voice. "And you might also stop plaguing me."

"Farou, I'll end by believing you know nothing about anything. Haven't you the slightest notion why Jane speaks with scorn and contumely of the men who have shared her bed?"

Farou appeared to be thinking.

"Yes, of course I have. It's natural."

"Oh!"

"It's the survival, an honourable one, of a sense of decency in the female. It's contrition. It's aspiration towards something better."

"Farou, you make me laugh."

He enveloped her in the light of his critical yellow eyes, as if she were his flock, his walled vegetable garden.

"It's you who don't begin to understand. You're much too ingenuous. You're a monster. And besides, you're in love with me, and that robs you of all discernment."

She put her arms round his neck and rubbed her little white nose against him.

"You're making me too hot," said Farou, unwinding her arms. "You are as logical and consistent as a third act. Let me work. Send Jane to me, and a glass of orange-ade, a grape or two, something light."

"Nice little second act? The bedroom scene?" Fanny suggested maliciously.

"Let me be, Fanny, let me be. No more jokes! You're the only ordinary woman I know. Mind you guard your prerogatives."

With a heavy yet gentle hand, he smoothed his wife's dark hair, and she asked him softly, with no insistence, whether he loved her.

"I really don't know, my dear."

"What do you mean?"

"No, I don't always notice that I love you. But if I stopped loving you, I would notice it at once. And I'd be very unhappy."

She looked up at him from below, deliberately insistent, knowing that an imploring look emphasised the whites of her dark eyes.

"Oh ho! very unhappy! Can you be very unhappy? You?"

"I trust not," he said with some anxiety." I never have been, have you?"

She lifted her shoulders in a gesture of uncertainty and shook her head.

"No. . . . No. . . ."

'No,' she repeated to herself. 'Worries, heaps of worries. The tricks you play me oftener than I deserve, probably. . . . Your filthy Farou temper, and my feeling of uselessness. But all that hardly counts. No. . . . No.'

"Handsome Farou! Unkind Farou! Unmannerly Farou!"

Deeply moved, she hummed the words in an undertone, so that he should not hear that the thread of her voice was wavering, like a fountain in the wind.

4

'VERY unhappy. . . . Can he ever be very unhappy? Or even sad? In any case, he's not unkind. But nobody has ever had cause to say, or to hear it said of him, that he is kind. Or cheerful, either. How little he resembles a man of the theatre! Yet he loves the theatre. . . . No, he doesn't love the theatre, he loves writing plays. Why am I so made that I associate his profession, his art, with a capricious female occupation? Not quite a female occupation, but a facile way of earning one's living. But if it were facile, a great many others would make a success of it. If Farou is successful, it must be because he is very gifted. Is he very gifted?'

Having arrived at the furthest limit of her conjectures, Fanny experienced much the same discomfort as she might from imagining too vividly a bullfight, say, or a haemorrhage, or a sudden fall. She extricated herself from a kind of magnetic vacuum, one which fascinated her, by resorting to her familiar calls.

"Jean, where are you? Jane! I've lost my lipstick again! Jane! Where is the big blue vase? I've brought some flowers up from down below."

Nobody answered her. She yawned, fatigued by an early rise that morning. She leaned over the brick parapet and gazed admiringly at the slope, then at the field path, then at the roadway lined with young plane-trees.

'All that long way! What a walk I've had! They'll be amazed.'

The scents of daybreak still hung in the air. The north-west wind was freshening the whole countryside, gathering up all the resinous scents, mingled with wild thyme from the little chain of grassy foothills and the bitter tang of a stunted oak coppice, to spill them over the slope on which stood the "Villa Dean".

"This house is deserted! Where are they all?"

A faint clinking of china sounded from the kitchen on the far side of the villa, where the outer wall was greenish and almost porous. Fanny saw herself alone among all the hideous, gaping, yellow-painted iron furniture, suddenly alone in this little known and little loved district. . . . She threw the large, already wilting bunch of pink flax and campanulas on to the table.

"Farou!" she called.

"Present, on his behalf!" answered Farou, so close to her that she shuddered.

"You're here? How did you get here?"

"What's wrong? Are the sheep in the corn again?"

He knew well enough that "Farou" is a name often given to sheepdogs, and deigned to make a joke of it.

He filled the hall doorway, standing there in his light clothes, informal but spruce, bare-headed, with a knotty stick in his hand. He started to laugh because Fanny, in her surprise, was gaping like a fish. She grew cross.

"Why are you laughing? A moment ago you weren't in the hall, because I've just fetched the big red vase from there! You've been for a walk. . . . No, you haven't, because I've just come up from the meadows below; where could you have been? You're not a needle, or a sylph. Are you listening, Farou? And—what wide nostrils you've got. I never noticed before how broad your nose was! Why are you making fun of me? Why can't you say something?"

He was laughing at her, showing the widely spaced teeth of a man predestined to be happy. On seeing the double row of his blood-red gums, Fanny lowered her voice and prepared to assume her "favoured retainer" expression.

"Have you finished?" asked Farou.

"Of course I've finished. You're not worth more!"

She saw fine weather signs in the depths of his eyes and in a low voice began one of those *Litanies Farouches*, the words and music of which she used to compose in days gone by, during the hours of satisfied love. "Colour of old amber. . . . Colour of angry gold. . . . Of the Moret nun's barley-sugar. . . ."

A cloud passed over the eyes she was praising and Farou blinked his tired eyelids.

"Ah, Farou . . ." sighed Fanny, flattered.

But she at once took hold of herself and cloaked her pleasure under an awkward, conventional modesty. Farou followed the direction of her glance, and saw his son, disguised and smartened by tightly belted blue over-alls. He fell back on his stock joke. "Cheese it, the Cops!"

"Oh, and there is one! Where have you come from, *Vergissmeinnicht*? Where have you come from, king-fisher? Where is Jane?"

"I don't know," Jean Farou replied politely.

"I hope you haven't been down to the village like that!"

"Blue jeans are all the rage," Jean replied in the same tone of voice.

Outwardly calm, he seemed to be shaking with a static impatience; the blue linen garment intensified the blue of his eyes, and the breeze raised a flame of golden hair along his forehead.

"You must admit he's becoming very good looking," Fanny whispered softly to her husband.

"Very," Farou curtly agreed. "But what a get-up!"

"Now, listen, you! Funds are low. I'm waiting until the last moment before renewing the boy's wardrobe. You know he won't really have a shirt to his back by the end of the holidays."

"Then wait no longer, Fanny. That bitch of an *Atalanta* is sold at last. Buy him silk pants—in moderation."

He held out a cheque and a letter which she could not read.

"Is it in English?"

"American, Madame. Fifty."

"Thousand?"

"*Yep*. And as for *Stolen Grapes*, that will be settled any time now. Touch wood!"

"Jean! Jean, come here!"

"I heard," said little Farou from afar. "Well done, Daddy! Thank you, Daddy!"

"Did it come this morning, my Farou? While I was down in the meadows? Blessed be the hand whence comes my bounty!"

Flushed with joy, she pushed back the black band from her right eye and bent to print a quick kiss on the strong, scented hand which still held the cheque and letter from America. On the dry knuckles she caught sight of greasy, purple stains and cried out, laughing like a child.

"Oh, you were with Jane, and got her to translate the letter. That's the ink from the typewriter she had in her room! I've caught you out!"

"Well!" said Farou, looking at his stained hands. "Well! My word, what an eye!"

"You can put that in your next play. I make you a present of it for your Branc-Ursine!"

She was convulsed with laughter as she lightly struck

Big Farou again and again with a long stalk of pink flax. She pirouetted round him, nimble and plump, and slightly out of breath. She stopped only when she caught little Farou's steely eye, filled with ascetic scorn.

'Jane is right,' she thought, offended. 'That boy's becoming impossible.'

"Jane!" she shouted in a piercing voice. "J-a-n-e!"

"Now what do you want her for?" grumbled Farou.

"I want her to come to the village with me, of course! Sign that cheque of yours, Farou, I shall be passing the little branch office of King's. And we'll bring back some nice sweet grocer's champagne and warm shortbread: in other words, we'll carry out a raid. J-a-n-e!"

Jane appeared, her hands over her ears. She was wearing a mauve linen dress, shrunk by frequent washing but kind to her tanned complexion and to her hair, lighter in colour than her forehead. She was doing her best to get a word in edgeways between Fanny's cries.

"How money . . . How money does affect you, Fanny! How you can . . . The butcher will hear you."

"I'll give him socks!" squealed Fanny. "I'll chuck his bundle of francs at him! Smack in his face, like that! Jean, just skip down to the garage and tell Fraisier to get the car out. Oh, my dears, it does me good! You're a trump, Big Farou! Jane, what would you like?"

"Me? Why, nothing . . . nothing. . . ."

"Do you hear her, Farou? Make her, Farou, do make her want something!"

She whirled round suddenly to call him to witness. Untouched by her overflowing joy, he had inclined his curly head with its thick, silver-threaded brown locks and seemed to be listening to some gentler sound, to have his mind on a less animated scene.

"What is it?" Fanny asked in a small voice.

Farou raised his eyes, which still held a faraway look.

"Off you go, off you go! And come back quickly. I'm already beginning to feel ravenous."

A large white rush hat and a big yellow linen hat were snatched from the pegs, and the two women ran off down the slope. Fanny pulled Jane by the hand, and Jane, ever responsive but rather detached, let her arm go limp, offering no resistance, and skilfully avoided stumbling or throwing her weight on Fanny. Farou watched them go down, his face still holding the gentle expression which, with him, denoted the most primitive innocence. He sensed that his son was approaching and his expression changed.

"Aren't you going with them?"

"No, daddy." And he added, "If you don't mind."

The pause before the respectful phrase was sufficiently long for Farou to interpret it as veiled insolence. He turned to look at his son, who was sitting sideways on the wall juggling with a pebble or two, and was about to speak gruffly to him as to a woman. He restrained himself as he looked more closely at the stranger born of his own loins, not yet fully grown, whose shape and careless attitude as he bent over the void were unquestionably virile, endowed with the overabundant virility that often emanates from a frail body and dominates its grace. Farou repressed his animosity and wisely put it behind him.

"What are you going to do?"

Jean Farou misinterpreted the question.

"Why, wait for them. They won't be long."

Farou pulled his hand from his pocket with an effort to brush that answer aside, then significantly changed the tone of his voice.

"No. What I mean is—what are you going to do?"

"Oh, I see."

As a gambit, he tried out a timid request.

"Would you let me go away—right away? You might find me something, say, with your friends the Secrestats, in the Argentine?"

Farou turned his head towards the steep path where a moment ago the yellow and mauve frocks were twirling like two flowerheads on the same stem as they floated downhill, and his handsome, mature, manly, countenance softened.

"It depends," he answered without enthusiasm. "It depends, of course, on the conditions under which I could . . . we could organise, arrange a visit abroad for you."

Jean was quick to seize upon this semi-acquiescence.

"Exactly! Besides, there's no hurry. If I may, as soon as we get back to Paris, I'll make an appointment to see the French Secrestats. There's the matter of my call-up, but by that time I should have managed to get in almost three years in South America of commercial life."

He was forcing his young voice, exaggerating the precision and speed of his words in order to show up a certain weakness which had dulled and slowed down his father's utterance. Each of them, looking at the other, felt loathing for an aspect of humanity different from his own. Farou was offended by this blue, metallic son, adorned with gold, piercingly sharp, studded with hard facets and mysterious refractions; while Jean blushed if he so much as touched the thick-skinned flabbiness of Big Farou, pliable as elastic, capricious, and as completely lacking in a sense of the future as any pleasure-loving woman.

Farou found no difficulty in remaining silent but a great deal in making the gesture of raising his heavy arm to his son's shoulder.

"Let's go a little way down to meet them."

'No. . . . No. . . .' Jean Farou protested inwardly, in revulsion from the muscular burden. 'No. . . . No. . . .'

Yet he bore the weight of the arm with painfully mixed feeling: the slightly hairy finger-joints hanging beside his cheek, with their mixed smell of tanned skin, tobacco, and scented lotion, undid his proud little boy's heart and tormented him with a terrible longing to cry, to kiss the dangling hand.

He triumphed over this, already bitterly aware that what is permissible in a child does not outrun childhood. He kept in step with his father and fell behind whenever the path became too narrow for the two of them to walk abreast.

5

' "IMPOSSIBLE" is putting it too strongly. I was un-
nerved by that cheque. I exaggerated far too much
the other day. He's a poor little boy with nothing to do,
and we none of us look after him as we should. He's not
impossible at all. He's even very sweet.'

"Jean, do you hear me?" Fanny said aloud. "You're
very sweet."

He turned his head in a vivacious manner, to give her
a fleeting smile and a nod as though she were some tire-
some acquaintance, and returned to his alert immobility.

"Jean, you won't be doing badly with four . . . no,
with three suits from Brennan's. I say three, because it's
better to have three suits and an overcoat than . . . Be
an angel, Jean Farou, and pick up my scissors."

He sprang up, pounced on the scissors, handed them
to Fanny, and with another leap was back in his seat.

"Don't you agree that it's better to have an overcoat?
You know I'm not flattering you, but Clara Cellerier is
sure to refer to you as a 'dashing horseman'. I don't
imitate her badly, eh? Eh, Jean Farou! What are you
staring at? What on earth are you looking at?"

"At a brown caterpillar," said Jean.

It was a lie. His burning blue eyes were fixed, unseeing,
on the yellow lichen of the wall. He was all ears, listening
intently to the expression—since the wind carried away
the actual words—of two voices conversing fifteen feet
below on the first terrace. Fanny, who sat sewing in her

usual place by the front door, could not even catch the
murmur of voices. Jean was mentally measuring the
distance—two to three paces—which separated him from
the brick parapet, and the width of the coarse, scrunchy
gravel. He also reckoned that an old hibiscus bush that
spreadeagled the parapet at the end of the upper terrace
would permit his head, invisible among its foliage, to
peer down on to the terrace below. The concentrated
effort of his calculations sharpened his tanned features,
rosy and dusted with freckles over the cheek-bones: he
kept his mouth tight shut and never batted an eyelash.
At length he took a deep breath, as if about to leap
forward, and shouted in a childish voice, "I'm quite willing to hold your skein of thread, Mamie, but it will cost
you an extra tie!" Then he bounded towards the hibiscus,
slid his head and shoulders noiselessly under the leaves,
allowing his forehead and eyes only to protrude over the
wall.

Dumbfounded, needle in the air, Fanny stared at him.
Eyes popping and mouth agape, she gave expression to
her astonishment with the ingenuousness Farou found so
amusing.

A moment later she left her seat and Jean, hearing her
move, motioned her to keep quiet with an imperious
wave of the arm behind his back. Whereupon she carefully stuck her needle into the linen she was embroider-
ing, tiptoed noiselessly forward, and joined her stepson
under the hibiscus.

Down below Farou stood talking to Jane. His loose-
fitting white garment was faintly tinged an acid, satirical
pink by reflection from a stray sunset cloud. He was conversing in short sentences as he sat side-saddle on the wall,
while looking out over the parched valley. He pushed
back his thick curly hair with one hand and let out a

"Phew" of exhaustion. Fanny thought that he must be saying, "This infernal heat!", or else, "I'll never be quit of that fourth act!" She found him much the same as usual, tired, handsome, and very dear to look upon. Jane, in her mauve dress, was holding some typed sheets of paper. She went up to Farou and held out a page to him, which he pushed away, laughing, and no doubt protesting, "Oh, no, that's enough!" But Jane persisted and Farou, who had risen to his feet, pushed her aside with a turn of the shoulder at once so familiar and so lacking in consideration that Fanny recognised the gesture, a bargee's gesture, used by Farou to reject a tie, a comb, a caress offered by a loving and conjugal hand. To her great surprise, Jane was not in the least put out as she leant laughingly against a ladder propped up against the wall. She was laughing wholeheartedly, arching her neck, raising her hands, and fluttering her fingers in the air; the sound of her laughter reached the upper terrace and, in the exclamation which brought it to an end, "Goodness gracious, what a lot of fuss about nothing!", Fanny recognised an intonation alien to Jane's manner of speaking.

'She's imitating me, my very words. . . .'

She turned to the young boy on the watch beside her. He was gripping the top of the wall with both hands to make sure he did not slip, testifying to his prowess and his experienced skill in watching, keeping silent, and taking in the situation. He seemed neither surprised, nor pained, and he held Fanny back merely by a masterful glance which prescribed silence, and dignity in attitude if not in action.

Below them Farou was not taking Jane's merriment at all well. She stopped laughing and her features resumed a look of unconcealed, unbridled hostility. She snatched at a twig, snapped it off and nibbled it while Farou was speaking in deep, measured tones, vibrating with threats, insolence, and carefully chosen insults. Then she interrupted him, yapped out a few brief words, twisted the twig she was nibbling, threw it in Farou's face and made off, with a somewhat theatrical leisureliness, in the direction of the steps.

"Quick, quick, back to your place!" was Jean Farou's hastily whispered order in Fanny's ear.

Hard boyish fingers propelled Fanny back as far as her basket *chaise longue*. When Farou, the first to appear, arrived at the top of the steps, Fanny sat holding the loose end of a skein of coarse thread, which Jean Farou, seated at her feet, was mischievously tangling like a cat.

"Touching family scene," scoffed Farou.

His yellow eyes were shining, clear and hard.

'He's in a bad mood,' thought Fanny.

She shivered and with difficulty shook herself free of her habitual feeling of security, still confused at having left behind under the foliage of the hibiscus all the facial and emotional accoutrements of a spy. At her feet Jean Farou, holding his hands out as a winder, began to sing in a piercing voice. 'He's going too far,' thought Fanny, and it was on him, in her indignation, that she almost vented a rebuking 'How dare you!'; but she caught in the boy's watchful eye as he glanced up at her 'We're not through yet', and she said nothing.

"Fanny," Big Farou continued in a gentler tone, "what I just said was stupid. Pay no attention to it."

By giving a slight twist to her lips, she contrived to check the tears which had no more than moistened her fine prominent eyes, and was disconcerted to find that her feelings for Farou were only those of unchanging adoration and gratitude, mingled with a desire to apologise and own up.

'No, no . . .' she protested, despite the kneeling boy, whose eyes never left her.

Then Jane in her turn appeared on the terrace, and Fanny's unease suddenly gave place to an attentiveness that imposed silence on the depths of her being. She recovered her ease of movement and speech, and secretly congratulated herself.

"Ah, there you are!" she exclaimed.

"What have I done now?" Jane asked. "Were you waiting for me? I wasn't far away."

"Yes . . . yes . . ." said Fanny lightly, shaking her head and her black band of hair.

She looked at Jane with curiosity.

'She too? With Farou? But how? Since when? Can it be true? I'm not hurt. It matters so little. It's true that I'm accustomed to it. There was that pretty Vivica, who danced in the third act of *Stolen Grapes*. And, just recently, little Asselin. Oh, it doesn't last long with Farou.'

But she remembered a certain pallor about Jane, her absent-minded and melancholy moods, the violence of her tears, so many things; but when?

'Oh, yes—the day when I read out that letter from which it appeared that Farou had "sacrificed himself" with little Asselin.'

Jane sat down, opened a book which happened to be lying on the scaly iron table, pretended to read, then raised her head to the grey sky which held a promise of rain.

"My dears, how quickly summer comes to an end! It would be very sweet of you, Jean, if you would fetch me my little sleeveless jacket which I left . . . er . . . which I left . . ."

"I know," said Jean, who dropped the skein and bolted.

Fanny, ever on the alert, still tingling from recent shocks, listened to Jane with amazement.

'But it's *my* book she's picked up! . . . But it's *my* stepson she's ordering about! It's in *my* house that . . .

She felt the blood pulsing gently, then more rapidly behind her ears till it constricted her throat, and she called to mind a time when she was jealous and moved to violence. Anxiously, she turned to look at Farou.

'Isn't he going to, oughtn't he to say something?'

But he was dreaming, his stomach pressed against the brick wall—huge, heavy, simple and preoccupied. He inclined his head and shoulders in Jane's direction.

"Is that a good book you're reading?"

"So so," she answered without moving.

Jean Farou brought the little sleeveless jacket, placed it over Jane's shoulders as if he were terrified of burning himself, and disappeared. The sound of cupboards being opened and spoons moved about announced dinner-time. No one spoke, and Fanny could have almost cried out for help, almost prayed that a state of deception and ignorance might return to her, or else fury, screams, some sort of free fight. . . . Farou yawned and announced, "I'm going to wash my hands", and Jane, rising suddenly, assumed her most girlish expression.

"Oh, the hot-house peaches in the refrigerator! They'll be frozen!"

She rushed away, overwhelming Fanny as she passed with a light emphatic kiss, which landed haphazardly and was received by Fanny without horror or displeasure.

*   *   *

She slept little, but did not toss and turn. With first light she could make out Farou asleep in the larger of the two beds. Still weary, she looked him over and then

gave no further thought to him, or to herself. She noticed
that he had indeed a broad nose dividing his wide spaced
eyes. 'They say it's a sign of a good memory.' A fresh
breeze was enough to make her shiver, for she had already
extended a fine bathing-beauty's leg from the bedclothes
before going to nestle in the other bed against a big,
motionless, unconscious warm body. She controlled the
automatic impulse, tucked up her leg again, and settled
down once more in bed.

'How absurd I am. Really one might think that Farou
was being unfaithful to me for the first time. He's had
any number of mistresses since he married me. Any
number!'

She began to count them over to herself in an undertone, and naming them left her unmoved and almost
in high spirits. Faint footsteps overhead, a woman's
stifled cough, told her that someone else was not sleeping
well or had awakened with the dawn.

'It's her. I'm certain it's her. She's not sleeping either.
She's waiting for daylight, she's waiting . . . What's
more, she's a young woman admirably suited to waiting,
despite her short-lived outbursts. What is she waiting
for? After all, we're a sensible young woman. We know
perfectly well that Farou . . .'

But at that very moment, her docile mood underwent a
disruptive change which, by telescoping a short period of
time, caused her to relive that August afternoon, with
its nap after a heavy meal and the dream of storm and
expectation in the midst of which she caught sight of
Jane furtively weeping. As she came out of the dream,
reality—as in the dream—had shown her Jane weeping
where she stood, hiding a tear. A tear, a single tear,
plucked and extinguished between two fingers like an
ember. Among so many resentful or passionate tears, this

was the only one whose pearly weight Fanny would have wished to ignore all her life long; also the only one which could make Fanny once more a new, rejuvenated, self-assured woman in the clear, breathable atmosphere of unhappiness.

Quietly she got out of bed, exercising as much skill and precaution as if she were moving in the dark. Farou sighed in his sleep and turned over, moulding the whole sheet over his body like a great fold of a wave. A score of times malicious gossip, and Farou's own carelessness, had forced Fanny to imagine that masculine body striving after pleasure and taming a soft feminine body. . . . Many a corner of her memory hid recollections of bitter little tears, sleepless nights, letters purloined from Farou and restored without his knowledge. Christian names, unknown handwriting, blurred sketches . . . Fair weather spells speedily followed, she could count of them, and awaited their coming with composure.

"I know nothing more worthy of admiration than Fanny Farou's arrogant indulgence towards her great tom-cat of a husband!" Clara Cellerier would exclaim at the top of her old woman's piercing pseudo-young voice.

'It isn't very difficult to be arrogant or even indulgent when you reign supreme over something, even if it be a betrayal. How long have I not been the only one in my house to suffer at the hands of Farou?'

With a twist of her arm she gathered up her cable of black hair, which now seemed inconvenient.

'Oh, all this hair! Three snips of the scissors . . .'

She envied Jane her short hair—silver, honey, barley—which the wind fluttered over her forehead.

'Well, Blondie must be finding the time drag up there. She weeps so easily. I must be badly in her way.'

She felt her cheeks reddening, pressed her clenched fist

against her teeth, and shot an angry glance at the sleeping man, whom the grey morning light, rosier every moment, did not disturb. Lying there on his back, mouth open and rounded, his whole face expressed an impressive simplicity. Fanny was seized by a contemptible fit of gaiety.

'You'd almost swear he was going to break into song!'

She scanned in detail Farou's broad nose, the flat space cleft by a vertical furrow which separated the eyebrows, the short straight lashes. The relaxed jaw was beginning to show signs of age, but the face itself, invigorated by an enigmatic happiness, the neck round as a tree trunk, the nest of tangled hair, displayed a serenity, suggestive of a faun or some mythological creature. Fanny turned away from the open mouth.

'He smells like a menagerie, before breakfast, like everyone else.'

Farou's large hand, palm uppermost, lay extended beyond an arm with veins like vine tendrils, and opened towards Fanny as though in trustful homage. In her surprise, she could almost have melted in tenderness over this nail-petalled flower.

'Ah, I must beware of everything now. I must keep myself in hand, think things over, come to a decision. . . .'

Tense with wariness, dully wrapped up in her brand new widowhood, with noiseless steps she made her way towards the bathroom.

6

"COME, Jean, don't lie there! Jean, get up! What's the matter? If you're not ill, I will not have you indulging in these antics another minute! Jean! You fell! . . . Did you have a fall?"

Fanny dared not shake him, but she felt indignant that the child should lie there on the bank beside the path, fully conscious, prone and pale as a stricken fawn. His long slender body straddled the top of the slope, his hair and feet dangling on either side. A strange colour made his face look almost green and served to accentuate the pallor beneath the lunular freckles on his tanned skin. Fanny could just catch sight of the moist blue gleam in his upturned eyes.

"Have a fall!" he murmured. "You may well say so, Mamie! I'll say I had a fall."

She lifted a limp hand that did not grasp her own.

"Where does it hurt you?"

"Nowhere, thanks."

He closed his eyes again and took a deep breath. As she looked him over uncertainly for traces of a fall or blood smear, Fanny could hardly help suspecting the inertia, the lifelessness, the very pallor of this secret-ridden child.

"You were a very long time in the village, Mamie. . . ."

He spoke in a monotone and did not open his eyes.

"I like that! With all the things I had to buy. . . . In any case, how do you know I've been a long time? And then, the mail wasn't sorted, so I had to wait. How was I to know that I'd find you on the roadside like a scythed flower! And then, there's exciting news. If you only knew what's in the telegram I've brought back for Farou! Ah, that's made you wake up, I see!"

Jean had just sat up without discomfort: but a sort of mauvish smudge persisted under his eyelids.

"A telegram from the Vaudeville! Now don't let on that you know about it before Farou has seen it! '*My dear master, return earliest, urgent start* Impossible Innocence . . .'"

"Lord, how I hate that title!" Jean muttered.

" '. . . *rehearsals. November first opening. Affectionate admiration. Silvestre.*'"

"It really reads 'My dear master' and 'affectionate admiration'! Oh, good God!"

"Why not? It's only proper."

"Most proper. And what about the 'option' on his next play promised by contract to Trick and Bavolet? What sort of a schemozzle has there been, I'd like to know, between them and Silvestre?"

"They're not ready."

"Not ready? As if that couple were the sort of team who wouldn't always be ready!"

He was becoming himself again, and expressed his conjectures in decisive tones.

'Everyone knows more about what's going on than I do,' thought Fanny.

"Well? Are we leaving?" little Farou asked after a pause.

"Yes, but don't let's talk of leaving. . . . Here comes Fraisier. Fraisier, carry my parcels up to the house. If the Master is not working, ask him to come down here and meet me; if he is working, don't disturb him."

"He's not working," Jean whispered behind the chauffeur's back.

"What are you saying?"

Fanny stared so savagely at her stepson that he lowered his eyes and sprang to his feet as though to avoid a blow. She stared him out of countenance as he stood there untidy, shamefaced, and sullied now by the knowingness he had vouchsafed.

"If he's not working, he'll come down here. I shall rest here, where the ground's level. You know he doesn't like sick people. Since you are feeling better, go and wash and make yourself tidy. I don't want him to see you in this state."

The child obeyed and climbed the hill path. He was struggling against shortness of breath after his fainting fit. Specks of humus and sand still clung to his fair hair, as to a youthful corpse risen from the dead.

Only when he had disappeared from view did Fanny feel any indulgence towards him.

'He's just a wretched young boy. At his age the change is so rapid from cad to hero to desperado . . .'

She elicited pride from having dealt with him judicially, and sat down to rest on the wooden bench beside the path. The sky, only partially cleared by the morning's rain, was about to open on the setting sun: mountains and tattered wisps of cloud shone with the same reddish violet, a special Franche Comté purple that rivals clematis and stock. Before she had turned her head round again, Farou was beside her.

"What's wrong, my Fanny? You're not ill? I wasn't working," he added. "There's so little needed now to finish it. . . . Some things must never be written down, they come of their own accord, just like that, written on the air, sung in the train, invented at the same time as a piece of stage-craft."

He was describing figures against the sky, and in his

yellow eyes and appeased features—as well as in the smell
and sensuous warmth of the body leaning over her—
Fanny recognised the complete state of well-being that
permeated Farou after love-making. She steeled herself
and did not burst into tears.

"All the same, you'll have to write them down in
double quick time, my dear Farou. Look. . . ."

He read the telegram, gave a couple of little neighing
snorts, both vindictive and satisfied, then frowned.

"I shan't have Charles Boyer, then . . . Bernstein'll
never release him."

"But Bernstein is so sweet."

"That's got nothing to do with it. Sweet . . . sweet!
This habit of talking about Bernstein as if he were a bull-
finch or a kitten! Sweet indeed! Jane!" he called, raising
his head.

"What do you want with Jane?"

"I want her because we're returning to Paris, of course.
A telegram to Blanchar! A telegram to Marsan! Oh, and
that infernal little Carette to play the barman. Quinson
has his address."

He tore at his hair with both hands and suddenly
relaxed.

"It's going to start all over again, this eternal hunt after
actors. . . . Thirty names, and when it comes to the point,
not a single one available! Jane! What the hell does that
girl get up to as soon as she's wanted? Re-doing her hair
again I suppose, or in a little pink apron making jam.
The Angel of the Hearth! The Good Genius of the
Vacuum Cleaner! Jane!"

He radiated ingratitude and a natural ferocity. Fanny
listened to him in silence, and, for the first time, overwhelmed. The yellow eyes came to rest on her.

"Well, Fanny! You don't look as if you had the

slightest notion that our whole coming year, and perhaps future ones as well, are now at the stake, my dear! Trick and Bavolet postponed! Upon my word, there is a God! Bestir yourself, my girl! Can we catch a train tonight? Jane!"

"No matter what it is, you're surely not going to make us catch the train at three in the morning, Big Farou? It has no sleeping berths and is always crowded with Swiss! Isn't that so, Fanny?"

Jane had come racing towards them, but without exerting herself unduly.

"At a pinch, you could travel on it alone."

At this there was a minor explosion.

"Alone! Since when have I travelled alone when it wasn't necessary? And once back in Paris, with the house shut up, and the gas to be turned on, and all the other chores. . . . Oh, well, do as you please. Oh, you women! After all, I'm very longsuffering!"

He lost patience, as he did each time he gave way, and went off up towards the house with a sweeping gesture that repudiated the two women.

"Let him go," said Jane quietly. "I'll reserve seats on the day train tomorrow. We'll be home by eight tomorrow evening, and from nine till midnight he can talk with Silvestre. What would he do with the whole afternoon to himself in Paris tomorrow? Like all men, he must always have things arranged for his own good despite his protestations. At all events, there'll be no Yvonne de Bray. . . . Oh, he ought to have had Yvonne de Bray."

She laughed excitedly.

"In another moment, the way you were going, Fanny, and he would have pinned us down to leaving tonight. 'Yes, my dear . . .' Fanny, I shall want Fraisier, to take the telegrams. I'll type them out at once. All we have to do is each to pack her own trunk and Farou's. If we could get hold of Jean again, I'd send him to the station. No, I'll do it quicker than he would. The washerwoman is late with some of the laundry. Fraisier can collect it while I'm in the post office."

She calmed down, and tactfully assumed a bright girlish manner.

"Fanny, I do so want you to have a marvellous gown for the dress rehearsal! Clear the decks for action! Just see my nostrils quivering!"

Fanny, unmoved, peered down into the valley, where the first autumn crocuses had sprung into flower after the rain. A low, slanting ray of light picked out the purple heather.

"It's odd," she said at last, "I thought I hated this country. Now that I know we shan't ever come back to it, I find it endearing."

She tried to summon up energy enough to hide her feelings, but a degrading meekness was all she could achieve.

"Don't regret it, Fanny. You'll find lovelier places. Don't listen to Farou next year. Next year . . ."

As she stood shoulder to shoulder with Fanny, she lowered her voice with a resentment that did not seem feigned. Fanny detected in Jane's voice a note of complicity, of an ill-will aimed solely at Farou. She accepted the support of the arm offered her, a flexible arm, tapering at the wrist like a serpent's neck and hollowed at the crook, soft, deft, officious.

'That too serviceable arm! But if I were to hate all the women who have been intimate with Farou, I should shake hands only with men.'

Her courage returned as her scruples left her and she

satisfied her self-respect by speaking to Jane in a rather superior tone.

"Jane, would you be so kind as to find the inventory of the furniture of the Villa Déan for me? Old Déan is such a fussy character."

Jane, who was holding her elbow as they climbed the steepest slope, answered with a vague yes, yes, while keeping one eye on the door of the study, from which came sounds of a typical Farou commotion—the slamming of cupboard doors, the scraping of a table across the parquet floor, and the plaintive grumble of a servant being scolded.

The evening and half the night were spent in an uproar. At eleven o'clock Farou took it into his head to revise a scene of the fourth act and to dictate it in the hall. His voice, which reverberated from one bare wall to another, his set look of an inspired madman, the hammer-strokes of his steps pounding up and down the creaky floorboards, the docile piety of Jane who was taking it down in shorthand, all combined to drive Fanny into exile on the terrace. The stillness of the night and the rising damp held a scent of reeds hanging in the evening air, together with the sickly vanilla of buddleias.

In front of the open door giant moths whirled like a grey snow flurry, and Jean Farou struck down the largest with sweeping blows of his hat. Sometimes he jumped straight up in the air like a cat, and Fanny's attention wavered between the child's graceful dance and the difficult, impromptu work which must not be interrupted. She admonished herself to be a coward and turned her head aside whenever Farou's face, as it passed through the rectangle of light falling over the terrace, reminded her that it was her duty to suffer.

'Another Farou play. . . . Uncertain manna. . . . What

shall I do in Paris? Does this present affair between him and Jane spell complete ruin for me, or is it a passing sickness which will work itself out as it came, without my noticing it?'

Her hand was touched by a warm cheek. Jean Farou had just sat down on the ground at her feet, in perfect silence.

"What do you want?" she asked in a low, irritated whisper.

"Nothing," said an invisible pair of lips.

"Are you unhappy?"

"Of course I am," the shadow admitted cautiously.

"You deserve to be."

"Am I complaining?"

"You're nothing but a little wretch."

"Oh, Mamie, you've no team spirit!"

The cheek, now damp, pressed against her hand.

"No," Fanny breathed with a touch of pride.

She was beginning to discover a firm spot, a small callus of lonely strength within herself, and she took as great exception to complaints as to conspiracy.

"What's all this nonsense, then? Get along with you!"

The toss of her head shook loose her hair and she felt it slither on to her back, cool as a snake.

"How lucky you are, Mamie," the shadow sighed.

She scraped the gravel with her foot.

"It's not a question of my luck! It's no concern of mine! You'll never get me to admit that I'm concerned in it. You're sixteen and a half, you're in love, you're unhappy. It's all perfectly normal. Sort it out for yourself."

"Sort it out, indeed, sort it out for yourself! Oh, Mamie, do you really consider that sound advice?"

They were whispering vehemently but with extreme

caution, prevented from giving their anger full rein by
Farou's pacing up and down; at times he would come
right through the front door out into the night, chewing
over some such phrase as "er . . . er . . . *Pull yourself
together, my good Didier . . . er . . . Be once more what you
were before this vile day dawned. . . .* No, that's nonsensical.
*Be once more the decent little chap who was brave enough to say
to me yesterday . . .*"

He took no notice of Jane as he dictated, and would
come striding out towards Fanny as if he would trample
her underfoot, unseeing. She had never cared for these
sudden attacks, rare as they were, of working in public,
which she likened to a form of exhibitionism.

"*Pull yourself together, my good Didier, I implore you!
Those are not your words, they are hers, which she has put into
your mouth . . . er . . . I implore you . . .* Oh, that's more than
enough! Why did you let me dictate such stuff, Jane?"

"What stuff?"

"*I implore you* and *Pull yourself together*—have you ever
called anyone *My good Didier*? As a matter of fact, I
believe you're quite capable of doing so. Just say 'My
good Farou!'"

Ears cocked, Fanny and Jean caught Jane's strangled,
unhappy little laugh.

"You've no wish, then, to call me 'My good Farou'?"

"None."

"*Didier, I implore you . . .* We mustn't forget that the
Vaudeville is a sort of popular theatre. *I implore you, pull
yourself together. . . .* By eleven forty-five the whole house
will be in a state of high expectancy. The end scene follows
as you have it typed. Good night! Fanny, I'm going to
bed!" Farou shouted.

Behind him, Jane gathered up the sheets after levelling
their edges, then replaced the cover on the typewriter

ready for the journey. She looked pale and sexless as a tired employee, and Fanny could discover no signs of secret triumph about her person, or even of familiar intimacy with love-making.

'Shall I never think of anything but her?' Fanny asked herself fearfully.

At that moment Jane looked up anxiously as though to catch her eye beyond the light of the room, and Fanny rose to her feet, leaving Jean Farou a crumpled, sheepish heap.

"Are you going up, Fanny?"

"Oh well, yes . . . I've already had enough of to-morrow's journey. . . . And all those Paris characters we shall have to see again. . . . Farou has kept you working late."

"It's my job. But it's unbelievable, all the fuss about that tag-end of the scene. It's becoming childish."

She was defending him and at the same time accusing him, with bad grace. She slipped her arm through Fanny's.

"Fanny, why do you never take my arm, but always let me take yours? I'm very tired, Fanny."

"With good reason. . . . You've been hard at it from early morning."

'As hard at it,' thought Fanny as she checked back, 'as a housemaid, courier, secretary, butler, plus half an hour of love-making—I'm being generous—into the bargain. It's true! I perfectly see the disadvantages of her situation, but wherein lie the advantages?'

She felt she was being rather coarse and this cheered her considerably. But her optimism faltered when, lying not far from Farou, who slept with the soft, flute-like whistling of a kettle on the boil, she found herself faced by the bluish screen of the uncurtained window. The previous evening it had been a blank; now, patterned with gold and very dark red, at the moment when, between rebellious eyelids, the gaze focusses by degrees on fantastic fairylands, the night-darkened window was decked with a rime of rising images at which Fanny stared, motionless, lying on a haycock of black hair, lulled by an invalid's hope.

'Is it no more than that? Is it no more than that?'

7

A<small>T</small> the moment of their departure she was the least cheerful, but they were all accustomed to Fanny's shivering clumsiness that caused her to linger at station entrances and slightly hampered her movements when getting into a motor car. When the time came to hand over the keys of the Villa Déan to the caretakers, she seemed to wake up; she tied the two ends of a scarf under one ear and crammed down her felt hat, already pushed out of shape by her large bun, to the very bridge of her nose. With hesitant steps, she wandered to and fro on the terrace and put a hand on the padlocked door.

"No, Fanny, no! You really haven't left anything behind," Jane called to her.

'I would like,' Fanny said to herself, 'I would like to start the summer all over again, fortified by the knowledge I now have. I should see the house in another light, and the landscape and the people and myself. These empty chairs already have a different look; this great gimcrack house is less hideous; the plan of the rooms and the two storeys is now clear to me, as though the front of the building had been blown in.'

She heard laughter and saw Jean Farou walking away, piled high, as a joke, with all their overcoats and looking just like a conical haystack on the move. She joined in their laughter, tripped and twisted her foot.

"It's always your butter ankles," Farou scolded.

"You'd do better to give her your hand," Jane retorted.

She brought up the rear, graceful in her girlish, pale blue silk waterproof. Farou stopped and waited for her. He slipped his hand through the tight white leather belt round Jane's waist and dragged her along.

"Gee-up! Ktt! Ktt! little blue horse!"

As always at the end of his holidays, he looked as if he were wearing borrowed clothes; his coat and waistcoat buttons undone, his hat pushed to the back of his head. A wiry tuft of hair curled above his forehead like the crest on a bull-calf. Jane took exception to his uncreased trousers and loosely knotted tie; but Farou, bright-eyed and grinning broadly, laughed and archly succeeded in scorning sartorial convention.

"Ktt! Ktt! little horse!"

'The innocence of it!' Fanny marvelled. 'And what was it she said to him just now? That he would do better to give me his hand. . . . How often in the past three years—no, four years—has she made the same kind of remark? I used to pay no attention to them. "You would do better to give her your hand!" '

The path was smothered in spider-webs; by seven-thirty the morning sun, still low and red, was not strong enough to absorb the dew. A sere and golden autumn was licking the feet of the lower hills like a flickering flame. As she passed, Fanny leaned over the kitchen-garden hedge and picked some mauve Michaelmas daisies she had scorned the day before.

In the train, Jane wanted to prepare "Fanny's corner". She unrolled the light kasha rug and slipped a paper knife between the pages of a brand new novel; but Fanny desired neither her attentions nor sleep.

"I'm quite comfortable, thank you, I'm quite comfortable," she repeated in a listless voice.

Her lovely, rather bovine eyes wandered over the

fields. A violet arabesque on the tips of her scarf and the bright lipstick on her mouth combined to make her fair-skinned brunette's complexion appear even whiter.

On the platform, Jean Farou promised to leave the wheel in the capable hands of Fraisier, promised not to drive on after nightfall, promised with speed and insincerity all that he was asked to promise.

"What newspaper would you like, Fanny?"

"None for the time being, thank you. I'm quite comfortable."

'And the best of it is that I'm not in the least uncomfortable,' she went on to herself.

The first little Franche Comté stations, their vines laden with tight bunches of black grapes, sped past the train. Farou read the papers after his fashion.

"They haven't announced it: it's not announced yet. . . ."

"What's that?" asked Fanny, startled out of her reverie.

"That it's gone into rehearsal, of course. Where are your wits?"

"You know what I'm like when you get me out of bed at five in the morning."

A curve in the track brought back to her line of vision the distant hill she was leaving, the square villa she would never see again. She leaned forward to watch one of the very few houses which, since her marriage, had sheltered her for two successive summers, slowly vanishing into the distance.

8

"HAS he had his lunch? I'm sure he hasn't lunched!"
"Of course he has! He said he'd have something
brought into the theatre. As if it were a habit of Farou's
to let himself starve! You make me laugh!"

"All the same, he's not been in bed by four in the
morning for the past three nights."

"So what? It's nothing unusual."

"Oh, what a Spartan you are! The Spartan Wife—that
fits you exactly. No one would guess it to look at you.
What's more, how grand, how noble! Such strength of
mind, such scorn of material comforts, such . . ."

The assembled women had not quite reached the stage
of begging for "a tiny corner, at the dressmakers' special
rehearsal", but they put on church-going, anguished
faces, intended for Farou *via* Fanny, and had already
assumed that air of cynical ecstasy which hovers ostentatiously round the playwright and actors of repute. They
did not mention Farou by name; they said "He", or else
"The Master".

'Well, what of it?' thought Fanny. '*He* has written a
play; yes, he's finished another play. If he were a cabinet-
maker, or if he had invented an electric cleaner, a fly-
swatter, a serum, would these women be bowed down as
if before a Christmas crêche?'

She preened her rather plump chin and kept silent,
hoping that these beggars for favours would go. But
assiduous as they were, they showed no concern for her.

"Is it a play on much the same lines as *Atalanta* and *No Woman about the House*?"

"The opening will be delayed, will it not? Mademoiselle Aubaret was saying to me, the day before yesterday, that . . ."

"Oh, really, Jane! You were saying, the day before yesterday?"

Fanny turned on Jane her Paris smile, well made-up and full-lipped, and Jane, whose fair hair lit up a corner of the room, was instantly extinguished.

"Who knows nothing, says nothing, Fanny. The Master leaves me in total ignorance, as he does you. But Madame Cellerier has ears everywhere."

Clara Cellerier was smoking, manly as a schoolboy, and exhaling with a long drawn "ph-e-e-w". A hat of chip straw, brimless and shaped like a small coal-scuttle, provided the only jarring note in a black and grey ensemble and endowed her with a chin unfamiliar to Fanny. The aged actress dressed daringly, with a kind of provincial bravado that for thirty years had inspired the respect of the *Comédie Française* audiences. That day she brought to Fanny's house one of those young actresses skilled in ringing up a playwright early in the morning, running into him in lifts, becoming speechless under his gaze, dropping a swift, awkward kiss on his hand—and dying of shame afterwards. Eager in the shadows, Clara Cellerier's protégée ardently hoped that Farou would return home for dinner. In silence this flaming blonde confined herself to afflicting her countenance with a consternation near to sobbing, when she heard that Farou, for the past week, had hardly slept, eaten, or come home.

"You'll soon find out what it's like, child, you'll soon find out for yourself what this last minute fever of rehearsals is really like," Clara Cellerier had promised her.

"Oh, Madame! I should be so happy to know. The slightest chance of my spending my time . . ."

Fanny considered her with a graciousness at once cold and familiar.

'I know her kind. Perhaps this one will get her small part—she's so persistent.'

Jane did not get to her feet to relieve the aspirant of her empty port glass.

A few of the women were waiting until it was time to go to dine.

'They'll leave,' thought Fanny, 'when it is convenient for them to go home or join their friends at a restaurant. They'll go away and say that they had "a very pleasant time at the Farous' ". I don't like that barrister's wife, or that high-class dressmaker, or the Farou cousin, who thinks it her duty, whenever she comes here, to make up her eyes and plaster herself with rouge which she wipes off again on the Métro stairs as soon as she possibly can. What a bore my house has become! And this furniture! It wouldn't even be acceptable as a set for the second act at the Scala! I ought to . . .'

A sort of metallic-green bird-woman, exposing a pair of sinewy legs, crossed the depressing square salon. Although a music-hall comedy star, the bird-woman ached to play in straight comedy, or tragedy. Even with its make-up, her little waif's face seemed the least important accessory of her acrobat's body. She strutted like a feather-legged pigeon, so accustomed was she to pacing huge stages, dragging dappled trains and a foam of feathers behind her, and shooting out at each step a small artificially cultivated, heart-shaped muscle on her sailor's calf. She seized Fanny's hands between her green gloves, emitted a sigh and a refined moan, and her respectfully sympathetic retreat put new life and a little gaiety into the company.

"The typical tart," said Clara Cellerier. "And to think she'll probably get the lead in Farou's next play *New Skin*!"

"She's a box-office draw," said Fanny.

"The contract isn't signed," said Jane.

The young actress shifted uneasily on her chair.

"Put on your cape now, child, I'm taking you off," Clara Cellerier ordered her.

The young actress took a few steps with hanging head, as if condemned to exile, and Clara Cellerier clasped Fanny's head between her hands, like an egg, in order to imprint a kiss upon her forehead.

"My dear Fanny, what have you done with your nonchalance?"

"My nonchalance?"

"Yes, your . . . How can I put it? Your *morbidezza*—what a pretty old-fashioned word!—your utter detachment. . . . I see that you are wide awake? Naturally, these last days are a great strain upon your nerves. But what a relief it will be, after the triumphant success! Lovely eyes so full of care . . ."

Gently, under her palms, she drew down Fanny's great eyelids, which reopened after the caress.

'The sharp old creature, she misses nothing!'

Fanny studied the bold features of the old trouper, her hard, precise make-up which austerely restored the faded contours of her face, her hat of chip straw, and her youthful black dress. . . . She was about to give some random reply when Farou entered the room. The young actress shut her eyes, as though wounded, parted her lips, and her hand flew to her throat. Farou's first glance was for her. Utterly exhausted, covered with dusty patches, his forehead damp and his collar a rag, he emerged from his rehearsal as if he had been taking part in a boxing match in a basement, or had fallen down the cellar steps. But at the sight of the young actress, the weak, happy smile of a convalescent spread over his face and he grew younger in a matter of seconds, by degrees, by leaps and bounds.

"What a state he's in!" sighed Clara Cellerier.

Impatiently Farou snapped his fingers at her. He was looking at the young actress and trying to put a name to her.

"Pour him out a glass of port," Clara Cellerier breathed into Fanny's ear.

Fanny shook her head, and with a tilt of her chin drew attention to Jane, who was fiercely crushing sugar into raw egg yolks before sprinkling them with marsala.

"By Jove," whispered Clara Cellerier, "whatever she's up to over there, Mademoiselle Aubaret doesn't appear to be getting much fun out of it!"

They exchanged a little laugh, which made Fanny feel slightly humiliated, and at last Farou spoke.

"Good day to you all! I beg your pardon, Clara, but I'm dead to the world. But surely that child there is young . . . Come now, I only know that she's the young . . ."

He was holding the young actress by the tip of her little finger, and was swinging the pretty, defenceless arm up and down.

"Young Inès Irrigoyen," Clara Cellerier prompted.

"A pretty name for a blonde!" Farou said.

"But it is my name," confessed the tremulous young woman.

"All right, all right, you're forgiven. But why on earth are you all standing about like this?"

"We're just off, we're just off," said Clara. "At such a time . . ."

Her well-timed false exit brought the lingerers to their feet and drove them out, even the Farou cousin. In their rear, Clara kept on repeating, as she pawed the ground, "Come along, come along, let's be going. . . . At a time like this . . ."

"Did it go all right?" Fanny asked.

A vindictive memory caused Farou to knit his brows, and his yellow eyes threatened a whole horde not present in the room.

"Yes, yes. . . . Oh, the swine! All the same, they were wonderful. . . . They will be wonderful. . . . Especially——"

"Especially who?" asked Clara avidly.

He eyed her with professional mistrust.

"Nearly all of them were wonderful."

"How lucky they are!" hazarded the fair-haired disciple. "Three lines in one of your plays, Master, would be a star part."

He laughed at her point blank, maliciously, to show that he was not to be taken in. Fanny knew that somewhat negroid smile, that open-faced grimace with wrinkled nose and grinning teeth, which Farou overdid in photographs and at important business discussions.

"Three lines? Would you care for them?"

As though seized with vertigo, the young woman called Inès clung to Clara's hand and held her breath.

"Three lines, and a nought after the three? The small part of the shorthand typist? . . . Eh? Eh? What's this abomination, Jane?"

He pushed aside the glass which Jane was holding out to him.

"Your raw egg concoction again? Pass it on to a consumptive, my dear. A small port, if you please."

He drank and his manner changed.

"Mademoiselle . . . Inès, will you kindly remember that the rehearsal is at one o'clock sharp," he said coldly. "Favier has the part, he will give it to you. Mademoiselle Biset threw it up this afternoon."

"Threw it up?" Clara Cellerier repeated ostentatiously. "My dear friend, what times we live in! Threw it up! Biset threw up a part?"

"Yes. Actually, I threw her out, if you prefer it."

Clara drew herself up like a soldier.

"Yes, I certainly prefer it! For the honour of the theatrical profession, I prefer it! Will the dress rehearsal be postponed, Farou? No? You'll open on the date fixed? That's splendid! Come, child. How happy you've made her, dear Master!"

She dragged away the fair young woman, who took great pains over her exit, stumbled a little, stammered, went all childish as she reached the open door and clapped her hands.

"Not bad, not bad," adjudicated Farou as he tore off his tie and collar. "She has the artificiality required for the part."

"There's also the concierge's daughter," Jane put in from the back of the room.

Stupefied, Fanny's eyes sought her out, and saw that she was pale, with dark-rimmed shining eyes.

"As for you," Farou replied quietly, "please go and tell the maid to run me a bath and put out a clean shirt and a pair of socks. And confine your theatrical accomplishments to those tasks."

Jane disappeared without a word, but slammed the door behind her.

"How can you speak to her like that?" said Fanny, embarrassed.

"Don't worry about it, Fanny-my-Poppet!"

He lay, bare-necked, in the hollow of the divan, and closed his eyes. He was exhausted and sure of himself, victorious in his repose.

"Are you going out again?" Fanny asked in a small voice.

"Certainly I'm going out again."

"Are you having dinner?"

"No. If I had dinner, I'd be too tired and I'd be dropping with sleep. I'll have something to eat when I get there."

"Are you pleased with it?"

"Fairly."

He limited himself to that brief word and she insisted no further. What could she have tried to find out? She knew some of the scenes of the play, the surprise ending she did not care for, the end of the second act about which Farou had asked her opinion with affected indifference. She felt constrained, and more than ever a stranger to her husband's professional life.

'There you are—almost twelve years of married life, and such an awkwardness existing between us, such difficulty in finding the right words.'

"You are lovely, standing there."

She gave a start, and hurriedly smiled at the handsome golden eyes that were staring at her.

"I thought you were asleep, Farou."

"You are lovely, but you look sad. Perhaps you are sad, after all."

He lifted a hand and let it fall back limp on to the divan.

"What an odd moment to choose, Farou!"

"Fanny, my dear, what makes you think that one

chooses? I have come from a desert," he added, rising and stretching his arms. "Oh, those people over there! One of them can play his principal scene only if he shows his right profile. If I make him change sides, he acts badly. One of the women plays her scene of despair with cropped hair glued down with brilliantine. If you could only see her rolling her head about on her lover's knees! No, no! And on top of that, Silvestre! What a menagerie! You have the lovely face of a human being."

He placed his heavy hands on Fanny's shoulders and took pleasure in studying the pale face with its round prominent eyeballs, which might have graced a lady of the harem. She suffered him to look upon her with profound uneasiness, pleasurable as sensual pain. The floor creaked and warned Fanny that Jane had just come into the room.

"I am glad to note," Farou said without turning round, "that sometimes you know how to close doors quietly, Jane."

He received no answer. Leaving Fanny, he walked vindictively towards Jane.

"Eh! Kindly imp of Dundee marmalade! You've calmed down now, it would seem."

Overwhelmed by fatigue, he laughed almost drunkenly, as if to get his own back for the lengthy arguments and muffled outbursts of the Punch and Judy show that had ebbed and flowed across the footlights.

"It seemed to me that you didn't take kindly to blonde actresses. Eh, Jane!"

Fanny went over to him and pulled him back as if he had been leaning over a chasm.

"Be quiet, Farou!" she begged hastily.

She kept her eye on Jane, an exasperated Jane, strangely pale and on the offensive.

"If you think that's going to stop me!" Farou said very loudly.

And Jane gathered herself together as if, fearing a blow, she was already trying to return it, while warding it off with white forehead and immaterial hair. A strange grimace distorted the childlike bow of her mouth and her eyes were filled with misery and hate.

"Jane!" Fanny cried, holding out her arms.

Her cry and gesture loosened the tensity of the frail body, whose hostile rigidity brought to Fanny's mind a young Fanny of long ago, bullied by Farou, and so closely resembling this enemy, this gallant, sheet-white woman.

"Go away!" Fanny ordered her husband. "Yes, you heard what I said. Go away. You've work to do elsewhere. And another time you'll vent your wrath on me, if you please, not on others. Not on others, at least not in front of me. . . . You're . . . you're impossible before a new play. In three days' time you'll be . . . you'll be feeling much better."

She stuttered a little and felt her chin trembling. For a very long time she had not known what it was like to be angry, and while struggling with herself she smiled vaguely, as do certain animals when they take pleasure in their own fury. Farou misinterpreted that smile and gave in with the grace of a guilty man.

"Dreadful!" he sighed. "I feel I'm dreadful! What a brute!"

He underlined the word and repeated it in a conciliatory tone. Fanny was recovering her breath and clenched her teeth to stop her chin from quivering.

"Jane, would you mind, please . . ." he began in a gentler tone.

But Fanny interrupted him.

"No, not tonight! Everything will be better tomorrow. Go to your rehearsal, and sharpen your claws on Tom, Dick and Harry, on Silvestre, on the programme seller, if you like, but leave us alone!"

"There are no programme sellers at rehearsals," said Farou shocked.

"Go, Farou, go to your bath, go!"

He left the room and Fanny immediately set about gathering up the empty port glasses and continued to talk so that Jane might remain silent awhile.

"Oh, good gracious! No really—really—what a ghastly profession his is! You know, in his present state, the small amount of port he's just drunk is enough to make him lose his self-control."

Meanwhile she thought: 'I escaped by the skin of my teeth! How could Jane let herself go like that? She was going to speak, shout, say things . . . especially . . .'

Having repowdered her face and redone her hair, Jane was applying lipstick to her mouth. Automatically she bit her lips, chewing the fresh rouge, then painted them again.

"Oh, you know," she said suddenly, "I could have answered him back quite easily! He may be Big Farou, but he doesn't frighten me. I've been through a lot worse!"

She cast defiant looks at the door which Farou had closed, and the words that fell from her lips were those of a quarrelsome woman of the streets, or a disgruntled workman. The little smooth grimace once more altered the shape of her mouth, and Fanny shivered, feeling lonely and uncomfortable.

"Jane, shall we have dinner? I hate these hysterical outbursts. We are alone. Jean has gone to the meeting of his 'Active Youth League'."

Jane took her arm. Her fingers, still tense, danced on Fanny's arm and she gave her an anonymous kiss behind the ear.

'Two months ago,' thought Fanny, 'I might have sat down to table alone, or I should have given the young woman a good dressing down. But now that I know they are guilty, I feel shy. . . .'

She was faced by a stoical companion who drank, ate and talked. But at moments Jane was transparent and speechless. Then Fanny was able to diagnose the passing of pain or anger, as she might have guessed from the face of a pregnant woman the secret movements of her child.

A little later in the evening Jean Farou came home. He smelt of tobacco and of a male scent which was not his own. He was still vibrating with the shouts uttered by a hundred insolent young throats around him and the senseless and vain words he had hurled into the smoky atmosphere. Dressed in new clothes, with a badly chosen tie, a peevish puffiness under his eyes, and a new shadow over his lip, Fanny compared him to a bruised fruit. His entrance broke in on the great silence, in which the two women had taken refuge with their needlework and reading, sitting almost elbow to elbow under the family lamp.

"Are you pleased with yourself? Did you yell your head off? Did you drink a lot of muck? Did you establish certain principles and throw out others? Are you feeling sick?"

Fanny did not wait for his answers; she was interposing herself between Jean Farou and Jane; but, unerring, Jean's gaze never left Jane's face. He turned to Fanny simply to enquire with his eyes, 'What's the matter with her? What's happened? What have you done to her?'

With a shrug of the shoulders, Fanny, at the limit of

her patience, replied: 'Oh, for goodness sake, leave me alone!'

Little Farou dared not speak to Jane, whose scorn kept him at a distance and who was separated from him even further by her attitude of monogamous repulsion.

"Yes," he said finally, without being aware that no one was asking him any more questions, "it was all very brilliant. We were a credit to our fathers. They would certainly not have disowned all the stupid things we said. What a bear garden!"

He had been changing since his return from the country: he was acquiring an assurance that depreciated and some-how lessened him. At times, Fanny, in an access of maternal affection, looked at him sadly.

"Is my father at the Vaudeville?"

"Of course," said Fanny.

"Are things going well over there?"

"So he says. Hasn't he taken you there yet?"

"No more than he has you, Mamie. And you, Jane?"

"No preferential treatment for me," Jane answered, her eyes on her book. "Since rehearsals started at the Vaudeville, I've heard scraps of readings, grinding of teeth, arguments between Silvestre and the stage de-signers. Really, Farou hides his work on the stage, as——"

"As a cat hides its retirements in the sand," said Fanny, who wanted them to laugh a little. "And really, I wonder why?"

"Because he's shy," said Jean.

Jane raised her head at the sound of this word, only to lower it again immediately with an evil little smile.

"You're not going to make me believe, Mamie, that you've never noticed that my father is shy?"

"I confess," said Fanny, annoyed, "that this . . .

characteristic, has never . . . precisely struck me up to
now."

But she spoke haltingly while she reflected.

"I believe you, Mamie, I can believe you quite easily.
Jane, most likely, can't have noticed it either."

This indirect attack did not ruffle Jane. Jean's glance
greedily devoured Jane's shoulders, her arms, Jane's
knees, Jane's hair; but in the inflamed blue of his smoke-
reddened eyes, Fanny read only a glutton's stare and
hopeless resentment.

'Perhaps he's beginning to hate her,' she thought.

Little by little he was losing his stepmother's goodwill
and was aware of it. Available for looking after his
material welfare, she still scolded him with a Nanny's
bluntness. "Have you at least cut your toenails and taken
your Eno's Fruit Salts? I know you! Your motto is 'Silk
socks and dubious feet'. 'Clean teeth and a coated
tongue.' "

But for nothing on earth would she have sat down
opposite those blue eyes, clairvoyant, technically trained
and intense in colour, to ask: 'Explain to me how you
know that your father is shy! Tell me exactly—you who
do not live with him, who talk to him so little, who are
not his ally—tell me what you claim to know, what
miraculously you do know of him!'

The mysterious and unhappy young creature shifted
from one leg to the other, picked up the newspapers,
shook an empty cigarette box; but Jane neither stirred,
nor took her eyes from her book, until she heard midnight strike on a distant clock.

"Well, what now? Are you both staying here?"

"Farou has enough to keep him busy all night. Silvestre
is keeping to his dates. Friday, the matinée for the dressmakers. Friday evening, dress rehearsal——"

"Saturday, twenty-four thousand francs box-office takings," continued Jean.

"*Inch'allah!*"

"Who came today, Mamie?"

"Various people," said Fanny laconically. "Clara, the Farou cousin, some other people—nobody much."

Jane, struck by the names of Clara and the Farou cousin, feared that of Inès Irrigoyen and advanced a peevish, aggressive countenance, but at that moment, Fanny did not even remember the fair-haired young woman.

"And on that, children, I'm going to bed."

"Me too," said Jane.

"Remarkable how . . . Remarkable unanimity," mocked Jean.

He had not dared to say 'solidarity'.

Jane heard him and took the offensive.

"Yes, indeed! Master-Little Farou, yes indeed! It is a remarkable solidarity! Have you any objections, Master Little-Farou?"

"Me? No. . . . Not at all. . . ."

Losing all his affronted child's swagger, little Farou gazed in terror at his first enemy.

"Hush, hush! Peace! Peace!" Fanny ordered softly. 'Oh, these Farous, how tired I am of them!'

She pushed Jean Farou towards his room. "Sleep well, child."

But at the moment when Jean turned on reaching the door, she could not prevent him from seeing Jane, in an attitude of deliberate frailty and defiance, leaning against her shoulder.

9

THE following days brought Fanny her full share of excitement, surprise and unexpected minor incidents. Esther Mérya, the star, caught cold; Henry Marsan sprained his ankle in a trap-door; a new set, vetoed by Farou and insisted upon by Silvestre, again delayed the dress rehearsal. At each fresh incident, Fanny remarked calmly: "The same thing happened with *Atalanta*. We had the same trouble with *Stolen Grapes*."

But Farou, forgetful, touchy, sick to death of his too often repeated lines, broke out in honest indignation.

"Where have you ever seen such a mess? Where? Do they go on like that in Berlin? Do they go on like that in London? Such a muddle! Such inefficiency! Such——"

"What about your little Irrigoyen? How is she getting along in all this?" asked Fanny, out of the blue.

"Who did you say? Oh, yes. She isn't doing anything, thank God! Biset has resumed her part."

"Really!" marvelled Fanny. She ceased to marvel as she noted in Jane a renewed and growing happiness which brightened her eyes, her complexion, the tone of her voice. At Fanny's slightest request, she hastened up: "What do you want, my Fanny?" like a golden-haired pink-and-white young girl, winged and busy as a bee. A little song, barely audible, never passed beyond her closed lips. Often, when addressed, even as she answered "What is it, Fanny?" her face betrayed the candour and hope of a betrothed bride.

At the same time, as soon as he turned his back on rehearsals, on experimental lighting, and on Esther Mérya's bedside, Farou recovered his sweet temper—which sometimes soared and sometimes plunged abysmally—as well as his pacified golden glance, even the scent which emanated from him when he was voluptuously satisfied, and Fanny became moody again. Treachery had left the lower levels and was creeping up on her again. Farou's pleasure ceased to be a passing phase, a caprice born in the street—of the street—of the theatre—gratified no matter where. She reached the point of childishly working out the grades of the adulterous hierarchy.

'The young Asselins, the Vivicas, the Irrigoyens and all the small fry are Jane's concern. She can storm, weep a little in corners and—if she dares—row with Farou. But what about Jane herself, my home, my poor domain of a woman who possesses nothing of her own?'

For the first time in her life, during sleepless nights, she longed for a room where she could have slept or lain awake alone. The flat contained only one spare room, which Jane occupied. Little Farou slept in a room which, had he not been there, would have been called "Madame's boudoir". At night, Fanny and her husband slept side by side. A single frame of English woodwork, of the Bing period, enclosed their twin beds. For years their tamed bodies had floated side by side during the night. Farou, unfaithful and a creature of habit, demanded Fanny's presence, her warm stillness, the spreading sheaf of her black hair into which he could thrust both fists and tumble it by stretching out a hand in the dark. His sleep required Fanny's slumbers, her prominent eyes so closely protected by the broad lids, the foolish expression her mouth assumed in sleep, and the whole of her utterly feminine body with its undulations, as she lay on her side, her elbows close to her knees.

"Nothing is more self-contained than you, when you're asleep," he would say to her.

'He used to call me a tramp, because I curled up like a retriever. He said that I must have once wandered along the high roads and slept in ditches.'

Sad and cowardly, then wise and dissembling, she relied on her face, rounded and soft as a child's, not to betray anything but deep emotions. She alternated between irritating unhappiness and a state of dreading anything in the nature of exterior upheavals, screams, confessions, convulsed faces and bodies.

Occasional visitors, whose appearance was as seasonal as that of starling or swallow, took her mind off the subject. They passed through the house—open to all and sundry—announcing that the stormy period of rehearsals was nearing its end and that the play was at last going to see the light of day. Fanny caught a glimpse of one of Farou's colleagues who specialised in recrimination. Behind a closed door she heard loud and tearful reproaches.

"No, old man, if you make a practice of pinching the subjects I'm working on, or of systematically taking up those I've staged more or less successfully, you should say so! Your *Impossible Innocence* is my *Woman Warrior*. Come now, nothing else than my *Woman Warrior*. What's that! Doesn't love belong to everyone who writes plays? I agree, old man, but it doesn't prevent similarities being there! Flers and Croisset are already shamelessly using my *Rosine*. You must admit that disaster dogs me!"

"Your plays are nothing but a disaster," replied Farou, who promptly became 'unkind to the man', as Fanny used to say.

Before her eyes passed young actresses who hushed their voices in order to instil ideas of intrigue into Farou's mind; resounding duennas, a very handsome young man who departed all swollen with tears, like a rain-drenched rose.

"What's the matter with him? What have you done to him, Farou? He's crying!"

Farou roared with laughter. "I should jolly well think he is crying! It's Crescent!"

"Who?"

"Crescent?"

"Who is Crescent?"

Farou raised his arms.

"Oh, it's just like you not to know the Crescent story! I haven't time to tell you now. Ask Jane!"

Fanny never knew the Crescent story. Finally came the crack reporters and photographers for advance publicity. For both species Farou sported his faun-in-the-sun grin, as he leant over his desk, resting on his fists. There came, separately, Henry Marsan and Esther Mérya, protagonists with bitter complaints about one another. There came unknown actors with faces like beadles, who having conscientiously and modestly rehearsed for a month, declared that they would not act "under such conditions".

"What conditions, Farou?"

Farou made a gesture of despotic indifference.

"I don't know. 'Under such conditions'—'In such circumstances'—'And this being the case'—they are compulsory and expletive formulas."

"Is it serious?"

"Not in the slightest, my Fanny. God, how simple you are! It's quite usual. They'll act, and act very well."

"Then what's the point?"

"Ah, what's the point! And what of vain imaginings, Fanny? And the need to increase their importance in my eyes and in their own?"

He changed his tone and spoke briefly.

"Fanny, you're coming the day after tomorrow to my last technical rehearsal. If you see my son, it would be kind of you to inform him that he can accompany you."

"And Jane?"

"She has been told."

'This,' thought Fanny, 'is a summons, not an invitation. Let us sort this out. Why does he adopt that tone when he decides to show me a new play? "Because he's shy," Jean Farou would say.'

"You will doubtless be pleased to note that I've toned down the safe scene. Branc-Ursine still steals the letters, but he commits the theft off-stage, in the next room."

Fanny suppressed a shriek of laughter and bit the inside of her mouth. Farou could only bring himself to talk to her about his plays by using a harsh, schoolmasterish tone.

'Because he's shy,' she thought promptly. 'That merciless child was right.'

But she began to laugh secretly. 'He commits the theft off-stage . . . that's delicious!'

"So that," Farou continued, as if he were at the blackboard, "the audience is sufficiently informed by seeing the bundle of papers in his hands, and silent action can be far more impressive than an exclamation. It's the curtain. Do you understand?" he concluded, relieved.

"Excellent, excellent!" approved Fanny. "Much better. Much less——"

"Yes, yes, I know," interrupted Farou. "Hop off to your 'final fitting', to your Fanny-fitting. Shall you be beautiful?"

She mimed an Andalusian belle, her eyes velvety under her black band of hair.

"Irresistible! Irresistible and discreet. Lace—skin under the lace—a red coral flan right in the middle of the corsage—your grandmother to the life!"

"Cheers! I'll make love to my grandmother!"

Long afterwards, she remembered how, that day, his glance had wandered, his right eyelid had twitched nervously, and how passionately he had longed for holidays, vulgarity, stupidities and celebrations—all of which could be perceived through the fog of exhaustion. He smiled at Fanny in a womanly way and lowered his voice.

"They say there's such a charming film at the *Aubert* . . ."

And she was just a little sorry for him, remembering that he was short of sleep, freedom, leisurely meals, fresh air, and that, nevertheless, he never shirked any professional responsibility or dreary task.

"You're not going *over there* this afternoon?"

"Not for my weight in gold! I'll only go there tonight. In any case, they rehearse better without me. I seem rather to put them off their stroke. Yes, I put them off their stroke," he repeated sadly. "It's strange—I can never help them right up to the end."

"Well have a rest and then dress yourself up to the nines—Jane, are you coming to my final fitting?" she called.

Jane emerged from the dining-room, her sleeves rolled up and an apron tied over her skirt, looking very pretty.

"Fanny, you're crazy! And what will the new maid do? She doesn't even know how to lay the table. You'd think that in her last job her employers never ate! And I'm also ironing my petticoats . . ."

She was waving an electric iron tethered to the end of its flex and Fanny went off alone.

She returned, tired out after playing the part of "the author's wife" in front of icy young saleswomen and lively, gushing old saleswomen crowned with red or white curls, bursting with false emotions and deadly tittle-tattle, and burning with an old-fashioned passion for the theatre, actors and smart plays. These asked a hundred questions, pausing miraculously on the verge of the most outrageous indiscretions. She liked those sly old know-alls, bristling with claws, as satanic and maternal as attendants in a special hell for the convalescent damned.

When Fanny returned home, the house smelt clean. A vinegary scent carried the news into the hall that Farou had relaxed in a bath. He was singing in the distance, going to and from his study to the once white bathroom, yellowing now and old-fashioned in its fittings.

The new maid, full of zeal for the first two days, was following the houseboy about, memorising the instructions he gave her in a low voice. With devoutly hushed footsteps, they circled the laid dining-room table as though it were a death bed. But Fanny already knew that, in the kitchen, the new servant smoked and stubbed out her cigarettes with her thimble. Never mind! This evening the house was like a home, provided with a master, adorned with a friend who was probably devoted to her and so little guilty, probably. . . . A need to be able to love in peace, to shut her eyes to things, to grow old, softened Fanny's heart.

> "When the season of crisis is again to the fore
> And Rip, Pierre Wolff and all the Bourdets
> Are on the rocks once more,
> And Mirande proudly awaits his encore . . ."

sang Farou, who was not superstitious.

A peal of laughter from Jane greeted his improvisation. Fanny had just put a large cardboard box on the bed before switching on the two dressing-table lamps. Against the lighted background of the bathroom she saw Farou in his shirt sleeves and Jane, protected by her maid's apron, rinsing out a shaving brush.

"What?" said Farou. "Isn't that a pretty song, then?"

"Stupid!" Jane replied in her angel voice.

"Ah! Really stupid?"

He pressed Jane against the wall, hiding her entirely with his tall thick-set body. Nothing could be seen of her but two small feet and a bare elbow resting on Farou's shoulder.

Placing his hand on her forehead, he tilted back her head and kissed her mouth in comfort, without lingering.

"And that—is also stupid?"

The young woman disguised as a servant shook herself free with an air of coquettish bravado, looked at herself in the mirror and answered in rather a husky voice: "It's worse than stupid, it's bungled."

She moved out of the clear background of the bathroom and Fanny trembled with fear. 'She'll see me—she's coming in here—she'll know that I've seen them.'

And she fled into the dining-room where, to keep herself in countenance, she was drinking a glass of water when Jane found her.

"Water before meals? Are you at last being sensible, Fanny? Have you just come back? Where is the dress?"

"I've brought it back."

"That's much safer. But don't drink so quickly! What's come over you?"

"I'm rather cold," said Fanny.

Jane took the half-filled glass from her.

"Cold? Ah, no, Fanny! Nothing so foolish, please!

No influenza before the first night! But I don't like the look of you at all, now you're back! Give me your hands!"

Fanny's hands allowed themselves to be roughly examined by two hands which retained the vinegary scent of Farou's bath; two dark grey eyes, steady and searching, looked straight into her own, seeking for signs of a possible illness. She coughed away a sob and tears rose to her eyes.

"Your throat! Of course! Aspirin, quinine, bed, hot drinks—Farou!"

"Leave him alone."

"Nonsense! Farou!"

He came, his cheeks and ears white with talcum powder and his little improvised song on his lips.

"She's ill," Jane cut him short.

"No," said Fanny struggling.

"No?" said Farou.

"She-really-is-ill!" affirmed Jane. "Big Farou, are you going *over there*? Then stop at the all-night chemist and send back by the car some English aspirin, a box of plasters and some tincture of methylene. I'll write it all down and you can give the list to Fraisier."

She left the room while Farou bent over Fanny, repeating: "Well, my Fanny? Well?"

'Ah! Well never mind—it's easier that way,' thought Fanny.

She gave Farou a slight, apologetic smile, closed her eyes and slipped full length on to the carpet.

Her sham fainting fit gave her respite and repose. Entrenched behind her closed eyelids, she listened to the sound of voices and rapid breathing. Farou picked her up bodily, clumsily, with powerful arms. She abandoned herself to those masculine arms, made to ravish and wound. She knew he would knock her feet as he went through the door, but that he would hold her firmly. Always that vinegary scent of bathwater. . . .

"Here, get out of the way so that I can pass," he said to Jane.

"I'm holding the door open to prevent it closing on you. Don't shake a fainting woman about in that way! Wait till I turn down the bed! Go and tell Henriette to fill a hot-water bottle!"

"Shall I telephone Doctor Moreau?"

"If you like. At the moment he can do no more than I can. The first thing to do is to get her conscious again quickly. There's nothing wrong with her lungs, her breathing is steady."

They spoke quickly, in whispers. Fanny prolonged this moment of secret watch, of relaxation, of false pretence. She had managed to let her head fall into a position that enhanced her beauty and the bedside light shed a rosy glow on her closed eyelids. A hand slid the flabby, burning hot-water bottle under her shoeless feet.

"It's boiling," said the maid's voice. "I will take off Madame's stockings."

"Then—shall I go?" asked Farou.

"Yes, go. Don't forget the chemist!"

"What a thing to say! Shall I 'phone from the Vaude-ville?"

"If you like. Personally, I think it's only a very minor complaint."

"But she doesn't usually suffer from minor complaints," said Farou, perplexed.

"That doesn't mean that she hasn't any right to have them, does it? Go quickly!"

As Jane's hand sought for the hooks of Fanny's dress, it lightly touched her breasts and Fanny could not repress the jerk of a fully conscious woman. Filled with shame, she opened her eyes.

"Ah, there you are!" said Jane. "There you are! Well, really!"

She wanted to laugh and instead burst into nervous tears. Forgetting the gesture that prostrated her, with her head rolling in Fanny's lap, her tears broadcast, Jane wept where she stood, quite simply, dabbing her eyes with her handkerchief. With one hand she made a sign.

'Wait, it will soon be over.'

She was not embarrassed by Fanny's big eyes, dark and expressionless, which were staring fixedly at her. She sat down on the bed and pushed back the band of black hair which fell across one white cheek.

"Now tell me. How did it happen?"

Fanny clenched her clasped hands and summoned all her strength in order to remain silent.

'If I speak, Jane will exclaim: "What! Because of that? Because of Farou and me? But that goes back to the dawn of time! But surely you're not making a fuss about that? But you yourself have said a score of times . . ." '

"You aren't in the family way, by any chance?"

Her words seemed so inappropriate to Fanny that she smiled.

"What was so funny in what I said? Do you think you are proof against all kinds of little Farous, boys or girls?"

"No," said Fanny, feeling extremely awkward. All that was most commonplace and sensitive in her nature considered for an instant the picture that moves all women— a child, indistinct and small. Fanny placed her hand on Jane's fair forehead and was hesitatingly imprudent. "It would . . . it wouldn't . . . Well, you wouldn't . . . mind if I gave birth to an unkind little Farou?"

Jane lowered her eyes. The dilated white nostrils, the quivering corners of her mouth, the chin which revealed the movements of her throat as she gulped with emotion —every feature in her face fought and triumphed.

"No," she said, opening her eyes again. "No," she repeated, refuting some claim which she was stifling. "No."

'I don't think she is lying,' Fanny decided.

She did not remove her hand which was stroking the fair hair. In this way she kept at a distance, at arm's length, a head and body which, in a muddled feeling of equality worthy of the harem, she would have taken into her arms and embraced.

A little later, she extorted the small perquisites of her position. She represented one of the two powers revered by domestic servants: sickness and wealth. She had a cup of clear soup, cold stewed apples soaked in red gravy from the joint, grapes, and magazines strewn on her bed. Jane remained in the salon so as not to tire "the invalid".

'What a fuss they're making of me,' thought Fanny.

She practised lying flat on her back, her bare arms flung out on the coverlet, seeking the cool air.

'I'm probably slightly feverish. No, the aspirin is making my head spin.'

A tide of sound, ebbing and flowing, approached and retreated, and with it rose and then receded a picture, whose significance she did not very clearly perceive at this particular time: Jane flattened against the wall, almost hidden by Farou's vast body. She fell asleep and awoke towards eleven o'clock. In a hushed voice, Jean Farou was asking Jane's permission to enter the room. Jane, on the threshold, was keeping him prudishly in his place.

"You'll tire her. This is hardly the place for a boy. Tomorrow, if she has a good night."

Rested by her short sleep, Fanny no longer enjoyed being treated as an invalid and called out:

"Yes, yes, you can come in! Sit there. There's nothing wrong with me, you know."

"Nothing?" protested Jane. "She fell like a log, look, just here where I'm standing! She had come back from her fitting, I hadn't even heard her come in and we were even thinking that she was rather late in returning."

Jean, who was already as bored as if he had been at a hospital sick bed, intelligently raised his head.

"Who do you mean by 'we'?"

"Your father and I. Your father didn't go to his rehearsal. His actresses were all with their dressmakers. He had a bath and a shave and titivated himself like a blushing bride. . . ."

But Jean was no longer listening. He had ostentatiously ceased to listen, and he remained silent when Jane left the room.

"I'm able to talk," Fanny said to him when they were alone. "What's more, I'm quite all right now. I stayed in bed because it's comfortable here and I don't want to look ugly at the dress rehearsal; people would think I'd got stage fright."

He did not answer. After a moment's silence, he stared point blank at Fanny and shot at her the words "And so?" in so pointed and bitterly searching a manner that she blushed.

"And so—what? And so—nothing!"

She tossed about in her bed and pushed up her pillow.

"And so," repeated Jean, "they were there when you came in?"

She did not answer, her eyes strenuously avoided the stony blue of the eyes that were tracking her down.

"And then? Then, you were . . . you fainted? How?"

His words summoned up for her the picture of the child lying on the slope of the hill, head and feet dangling limp, the fair hair spattered with grit. But now the child had become this stranger, mad with grief, selfishly drunk with the need to hurt himself more and ever more. No shadow of pity moistened the blue eyes which questioned her, heedless of her feelings, and on the innocent mouth there trembled but one shameful question—the same, ever the same.

"They were—where?" he stammered.

She could never have believed that he would come to this.

No shadow of pity. She turned her head sideways on the pillow to hide her tears.

"When you came in, were they . . .?"

Between her lashes, clotted with her tears, she could see the child whom she had looked after, in sickness and health, who had grown up at her side for more than ten years. Obsessed with his first sorrow, he lived only to nourish it.

'How cruel is a child without hope!' Fanny said to herself. And her tears, flowing more easily, hid from her the fair face and the bitter curiosity of the blue eyes.

"Were they in here?"

As she was silent, he made a movement of angry impatience in which was apparent his contempt for tears.

"If I were you, Mamie . . ."

Jean's dramatic, threatening gesture which brought him to his feet was redeemed by a child-like haughtiness.

'A child,' thought Fanny. 'A child that I brought up. He was so gentle.'

She exaggerated the common sentimental links of the past in order to increase her tears; but all the new, recently awakened elements in her did not tolerate this procedure for long.

'Brought up! We'll go into that later. And as for his gentleness! He hasn't a shred of pity for anything, not even at this very moment for the woman he loves.'

Contact with this ulcerated child was calming her and when she spoke her voice was steady.

"You will never be me, child. Don't think you ever will be. And let me rest now. Good night, child, good night."

But he did not go away. His glance wandered over all the surrounding objects and seemed to call for help, witnesses, allies, a universal clamour. He rose, with swift obedience, only at the sound of Jane's voice.

"This late visit has lasted very long. Isn't he tiring you, Fanny?"

"A little."

"Jean? Do you hear? Clear out at once, child."

He went out of the door, carefully avoiding contact with Jane, and Fanny, delivered from the aggressive child, from his rigid, frenzied mind, which battered itself against the very walls, was able to breathe again.

The solitude and the silence were broken only by street noises, and by the coming and going of Jane, tall and luminous, and by the hardly perceptible breath of air which carried to the bedside the rhythm of her dress and her unctuous, slave-girl movements.

A lamp in the avenue below served as a nightlight. Open and ghostly, Farou's bed also lit up the room.

In its early stages, insomnia is almost an oasis in which those who have to think or suffer darkly take refuge. For the past three hours, Fanny had been longing for darkness and, precisely, for insomnia. All they gave her was the vivid picture in natural colours of a group pressed against the wall of the bathroom. She examined it in detail—the bare arm resting on the masculine shoulder, Farou's hair like a bunch of mistletoe against the wall, two corners of the apron fluttering. In short, nothing very terrible, nothing indecent, nothing sensual, which would justify the presence in Fanny's breast of those uneven heart beats, that imagined hardening of the heart, not the uneasiness and exaggerated fear that the pair had guessed her presence there.

'I must speak to Farou. To Farou, or to Jane? To Farou and Jane.'

She no longer recognised herself.

"Your'e much too simple," Farou would say. "You're a monster."

'Where was this Fanny, this monster?'

'Yes, I must speak to Farou first. No screams, no rows, just make him straightforwardly face up to the situation. . . . Come, that's impossible! We're no longer very young lovers; I shall therefore not take the line of physical jealousy which only enters into it in the very smallest degree.'

But an elaboration of that very small degree reminded her of Farou's good nourishing healthy mouth and the breath of his nostrils when he prolonged a tenacious kiss. She sat up abruptly, switched on the light and seized a mirror from the bedside table. The expression of an angry woman superimposed on a gentle face, endowed her with a double chin and a pouting lower lip, which she corrected. Except for her fine obstinate eyes, she considered that she looked ugly, but the evidence of her own violent feelings did not displease her.

'I can still lose my temper,' she thought, as she might have said during a siege, "Ah, we've still got a three months' stock of sugar!"

She smoothed her cheeks and her chin with her hand, and pushed away and settled her angry face into the background. 'In case of need, you never know.' She became quieter, with her sense of security restored through having seen and touched on her face, unchanged and ready for all emergencies, the innate savagery of the female species. A wave of loyalty brought about a truce.

'Later. In any case, after the dress rehearsal.'

So she turned out the light like a good little girl and when Farou came home, towards three o'clock in the morning, she remained motionless beneath her hair and peeped at him.

In the gloom, he wandered about aimlessly, coughing with fatigue and nervous exhaustion. Then he cast aside his garments like a defeated warrior. His broad back was bowed when he ceased to think about it and the weight of his arms dragged his shoulders forward. At the sight of this physical distress she, an inalienable ally of other days, nestling under her great curtain of black hair, nearly flew to his rescue, to offer beverages, smiles, words, all the consolations tested and found worthy during the past ten years. She controlled herself, suffered strangely, and feigned sleep.

10

"WILL anyone else but us be there, Farou?"
"Of course. Cellerier is coming along. I couldn't
refuse her."

"Why?"

"She has a certain influence—*ex officio!*—at the
Comédie Française! If the . . ."

"Wherever she goes she pretends she's the power
behind the throne," interpolated Jane.

"—if *Stolen Grapes* goes from the *Gymnase*, where it's
been stuck for three years, to the *Français*, I'd rather have
Cellerier on my side."

"Oh, yes. . . . And who else?"

"Their Ladyships, the dressmakers, their Lordships,
the dress-designers. The bootmaker. An American agent.
A couple of fellows from the German theatres. Photographers. Silvestre is also bringing some people. And
Van Dongen, because he's painting Esther Mérya's
portrait."

"I see," said Fanny, annoyed. "In other words, the
dressmaker's show! The whole of Paris. You should
have warned me. Oh, that telephone!"

Farou looked at his wife in surprise. He had never
before seen her nervous or temperamental on the
occasion of a new play. The telephone had kept Jane
with one elbow on the table and the receiver at her ear
since morning.

"The critic of the *Echo de la Péripherie* is asking for a
seat at the second performance," Jane transmitted.

Farou did not deign to reply. Egotistically and unin-
terruptedly idle, he had spent a painful, interminable
afternoon.

"Why didn't you go *over there* today?"

His smile was forced. "Because no one needs me any
longer. Jane, find out who has just rung the door-bell.
Ernest is so stupid. After that, get Silvestre's office for
me. What's been done about the flowers? Has anyone
thought about Esther's red roses?"

"Yes," said Jane.

"And Marsan's cigars and Carette's note-case?"

"Yes," said Jane.

"Abel Hermant's seat in the dress circle? Have you
seen to——?"

"Yes," said Jane, "exchanged for his favourite lower
box."

"What are those papers under the crystal paper-
weight?"

"Requests for seats, of course."

Farou became nervously fussy. "But I haven't seen
them! You must always show them to me—always! Why
didn't you show them to me before?"

Jane held the papers out to him and he pushed them
away. Fanny listened silently.

"Is that rain you can hear?" asked Farou suddenly.

"Yes," said Jane, "but the glass is going up."

"What's the time?" asked Fanny in the midst of a
silence.

"Oh, Fanny!" said Farou through clenched teeth. "It's
always too early! Esther's famous costume change in the
second act will be enough to land us in for an hour's
fitting, screams and hysterics this evening. . . . We're
having something to eat beforehand, I suppose? If Jean
doesn't get back in time, you are not to wait for him."

"Jean will meet us at the Vaudeville," said Fanny.

"And where is he dining?"

"With his committee."

"He's on a committee?"

"He's seventeen."

As usual, whenever Fanny showed signs of a sense of humour, Farou raised his eyebrows and was careful not to smile.

"Had I known that there were going to be so many people, I would have dressed," said Fanny. "Will Silvestre be in front?"

"Yes," replied Farou, "and also on the stage and also in his office, not to mention the flies and the prompt box."

"What does he say about the play?"

"I don't know."

"What? You don't know?"

"No. We're no longer on speaking terms."

"But you never told me! Why?"

"We're on the eve of a dress rehearsal. We've been rehearsing for forty days. He's the producer and I'm the author. There's no other reason."

He was tapping the windowpanes streaked with long tears of rain. He yawned plaintively.

"To have finished a play is not as amusing as one might think."

*   *   *

On the stage, with the curtain up, an endless argument was in progress between the stage hands and the stage manager. It had been going on for half an hour and might well go on for ever. The flute-like voice of the portly chief property man maintained a courteous tone and vocabulary. The stage manager, who looked like Barrès, took up the challenge and exhibited an invincible

politeness. In a lower box, Jane and Fanny already knew
by heart the details of the set for the first act, notable for
its genuine antique furniture, English silver and "real"
bound books, and they retreated to the back of the box,
chins nestling in their fur collars, shoulders hunched, as
on a station platform. Towards half-past nine, Jean
Farou slipped in beside them and asked, "Hasn't it begun
yet?" and received uncertain signs in reply. Interrupting
his dialogue, the stage manager turned towards the
auditorium and addressed the black vacuum and the
vague parallel rows of seat covers.

"Is Monsieur Silvestre in the house?"

After what seemed to be a very long pause, a sentence
floated down from a tenor-voiced seraph, invisible and
flying at a great height.

"Not here yet!"

The rain pattered steadily on the dome of the theatre.

"What are they doing?" asked Jean.

"Waiting!" answered Jane. "Oh, there's Farou!"

The stage made him look taller. He exchanged a few
words with the impassive stage manager, took the bloated
and floating chief property man into a corner. The latter
disappeared and returned with two skinny stage hands.
Thanks to their ministrations, a blue settee flanked by a
Chinese table disappeared and a ministerial desk and two
chairs took their place. Then the stage manager swept
back the Barrès-like lock of hair, put on his hat and left
the stage. From a vast basket presented to him by the
property man, Farou fished out a little Louis XIV wall
clock, a Japanese vase, a desk candlestick, which appeared
to be made of silver, and a morocco-bound blotting pad.
He placed the ornaments here and there, ruffled up the
artificial roses in a vase, then he stepped back to judge the
effect, altered the position of a piece of furniture and

readjusted the angle of a flower. Fanny watched this frivolous task unsympathetically, as if she had been watching Farou make women's hats, or embroider on the tambour. Jane touched her arm.

"You'll see—they'll forget to put the stick of sealing wax into the drawer."

Fanny noted that she was serious and attentive, and jealously tried to imitate her.

A white-gloved hand rose from a scrum of people clustered round the cameras in the middle of the auditorium.

"It's Cellerier, to let you know she's here," said Jane.

"Cellerier and who else?"

"People she brought with her, no doubt."

"What cheek!" said Jean.

"The first hands from the couture houses are further on, under the dress circle. Therefore Mérya is dressed and so is Dorilys. I therefore wonder what they're waiting for?"

She was biting her thumbnail. Fanny, overcome by an attack of recurrent yawns, gathered her coat about her shoulders and crossed it over her legs. Jean Farou left the box and came back with some whitish sweets, tasting of old vinegar. With little sideways dance-steps, the guests slipped between the rows of the stalls and greeted each other in low voices, as if in church.

From gaping boxes, which Fanny had believed empty, escaped sounds of a cough, a laugh, the snap of a bag closing.

On the set, between two leaves of the folding doors, a woman's head peeped out, shining with all the colours of a bouquet, and was withdrawn immediately.

"It's Mérya," said Jane in a low respectful voice.

"She's blonde now," remarked Jean.

"And a superb make-up. Did you have time to notice it?"

"Yes. Luminous. She looks ten years younger. At least, so it seemed to me."

They whispered feverishly. In the uncomfortable box, Jean leaned towards Jane, touching her with his shoulder and knee and inhaling an atmosphere saturated with her scent and her blonde warmth. He relaxed in the darkness, but stifled a little piercing laugh when his father crossed the set with a Spanish shawl over his arm.

"Ah, there's Marsan with Farou. Do you like Marsan's smoking jacket?"

"You can't like a smoking jacket. Why is he wearing one?"

"He's screamingly funny," decreed Jean from the height of his new suit.

"Fanny, do you remember your wild attack of giggles at the dress rehearsal of *Atalanta*?"

"My wild attack of giggles?"

"Yes, because of Grault's smoking jacket, his seducer's jacket of bottle-green ottoman silk, my dear! You just couldn't stop."

'My wild attack of giggles . . . I couldn't stop. Yes, I still want to laugh irrepressibly. I shall get over the state I'm in. You get over it, like an illness. I want to——'

"Mérya is making her entrance," whispered Jane. "Oh, that is a lovely dress! Just look at Mérya's dress. Fanny—eh?"

"Black is always distinguished."

"Will you go round and see Esther Mérya in her dressing-room after the first act, Mamie? Can I go with you?"

"No, no," said Fanny quickly, gathering her coat closely about her and contracting her breasts. "I shan't go. You can go with your father."

"Her real name is Mayer, isn't it, Mamie?"

"Of course."

As he bathed in the artificial light of the theatre, she saw the young boy's face glow, in spite of himself, the moment a couple of actors' faces in their traditional make-up appeared. He professed extreme coldness and distaste for Farou's profession, but in the presence of actors and actresses, grease paint, stifling boxes, the preparation and celebration of theatrical rites, he became once more a dazzled child.

"Farou is green about the gills," remarked Jane.

"In contrast," said Fanny, "Marsan has put on a suntan foundation. What a queer idea!"

"It gives a virile effect."

"Really?" asked Jean anxiously.

Fanny smiled as she noticed how simple he remained beneath his passion and hostility and how much importance he attached to Jane's slightest word. The curtain fell; a cold voice requested silence and added: "Persons not concerned with the play are asked to leave the stage."

"Who's speaking?" enquired Fanny.

"The box at the back of the theatre. The one with the yawning black cavern. It's Silvestre, who has just arrived. It's Father he means by 'persons not concerned with the play'."

The "fireman" struck twelve quick blows on the boards, then three solemn ones; a lazy little roll of dust swept along the surface of the floor under the curtain; the imposing furniture reappeared and the rehearsal began. Fanny leaned her head against the partition of the box and closed her eyes in order to listen. She opened them at a muffled exclamation from Jane.

"Oh, her scream misfired badly! What luck it's today and not tomorrow that she's muffed it! But in such an experienced actress, it's inexcusable. Farou must be simply furious! What do you think, Fanny?"

Fanny said nothing. Dumbfounded, she was emerging from a deep sleep which had appeared to be of short duration. 'Is it possible? I was asleep!' She gauged the isolating depth of her anxiety. Following suit, she repeated as the curtain fell: "It's really inexcusable!"

The auditorium was once more faintly illuminated. Palid, Jane was furiously biting her thumbnail. The door of the box opened under Clara Cellerier's gloved fist.

"Nothing serious, children!" she cried. "Only she must be careful tomorrow. An old warhorse like me knows why these things happen, these purely vocal accidents. The heat of the dressing-rooms and fatigue as well—I grant you fatigue. If Mérya had brought her voice a little more forward—d'you see? 'Hin, hin, hin,' like that!—it would never have cracked. Ouf! That's over!"

She sat down. The weak diffused light deprived her of her high colour and reduced her face down to the great shadowy holes of the eyes and the deep ravine of her mouth. For a few moments, Fanny imagined that her sleep had lasted long enough to age Clara Cellerier by twenty years.

"Let's talk about the play. By Jingo, what a masterpiece! That direct manner of entering straight into the plot, eh? Farou is a thruster! What an attack! I must confess that Marsan is first-rate. And the rogue remains a handsome devil. Between you and me, Fanny, when Mérya despairingly answers him: 'So many women have come to this office to beg you to save them, but I shall not leave it until I have ruined one or other of us,' don't you think that—gives it away a little too much?"

In the shadow, Fanny blushed; that dialogue had not disturbed her sleep. Jane forestalled her and answered with some heat, "Oh, Madame, a woman like the beautiful Madame Houcquart could not express herself in any other way. She's sure enough of herself to be in a position to unmask her batteries."

"Madame Houcquart is neither an inexperienced girl nor an *ingénue*," insisted Jean. "She doesn't demean herself by trying to play canny with a fellow like Branc-Ursine! Does she, Mamie?"

"You make my head whirl, the lot of you! I shall have to see the play through at least twice. I'm not as quick-witted as you," said Fanny out of cowardice.

She was dreading Farou's arrival; he came in almost immediately. He no longer seemed irritated, or worried, or even disappointed. Perhaps he felt already that languorous distaste which, after the first performance, kept him away from theatres where his plays were running.

"How do you do, Clara? It went well, didn't it, except when Mérya's voice went—a purely material mishap!"

Clara hung on to his shoulders and gave him her accolade. "What a masterpiece! What a structure! Real Farou granite!"

Farou tried to catch Fanny's eye.

"Oh," he conceded limply, "perhaps its only conglomerate. Fanny—you like it? Or not?"

She took his hands, pressed them and tried to satisfy him by a fervent silence.

"You shall tell me later. You are my stern little judge. I'm all of a tremble."

He was joking uneasily and Fanny thought he lacked his usual arrogance. She hated anything which resembled humility in Farou and took it out on her stepson.

"Well, Jean! Aren't you saying anything to Big Farou? You were enthusiastic enough just now! I could hardly control them," she said, indicating Jean and Jane.

"Oh, bravo, Father, bravo!" Jean applauded with affectation.

"Yes?" said Farou absent-mindedly. "Let's wait for the end. You're very sweet. Whereupon, children, I return to my stoking."

"If Marsan could hear you!" spluttered Clara.

In the gloom, her joyous laugh carved out the black, cavernous grin of a skull.

In the orchestra pit the photographers erected their limp magnesium balloons and Clara yawned.

"They'll be a long time. What about going outside to smoke a cigarette and drink a grog?"

"No, no," said Fanny quickly.

She corrected herself. "Not I, at least, I'm chilly, on edge. You three go whilst I rest. Yes, I insist, go!"

Left alone, she again leant her head against the partition and waited. Her sorrow was unsatisfactory. At times she would have preferred a young girl's grief, shrill and distraught, outside all self-respect, while at others she regretted her light-heartedness of the previous year and the bitter little mystery of the absolutions she granted Farou. She could not forgive her sorrow for being bearable and for taking its place, between despair and indifference, in a spiritual region which allowed of diversions, pleasures, scruples, and compensations. She was ceaselessly surprised that treachery had not changed Farou in her eyes and that Jane herself—'Except that I cannot bear *that*, I wish her no ill. At least I don't think I bear her any ill will.'

Clara Cellerier returned before Jane.

"Were you asleep, lovely darkling! I'll leave you. No? Let me tell you the local gossip, young woman! Marsan is starting a boil and a temperature. Up aloft, Dorilys and Biset are saying—saying! they're yelling—that Choquart only gave them a job here to have both of them conveniently at his disposal. If you could have seen Farou restoring peace! He held Dorilys with one arm and Biset with the other: you can well imagine they took advantage of the situation, especially Dorilys. It was enough to make you die of laughter."

'When one has no friends,' thought Fanny, 'from whom does one seek advice? From no one. And anyway, of what value is a friend's advice? This old Clara would give me advice in accordance with tradition, her tradition, in a manner it makes me sick to think of it. She would give me Francillon's or Mimi's advice."

"It has stopped raining!" exclaimed Jane. "I knew that the glass wasn't lying! It's fine and warm."

She brought back with her fresh air with a touch of damp in it, and the sooty scent of Paris rain. Her cold hand immediately sought Fanny's.

"They're starting, Fanny. Be off, Madame Cellerier! Silvestre said he would decapitate anyone who opened a door or put down a seat after the curtain was up! The same set is used for the second and third acts, so one can hope that by two o'clock at the very latest . . . I left Jean Farou with one of the Silvestre boys, but as they are twins, I can't tell you which it was."

She bent over Fanny, peering at her under the brim of her hat.

"I don't know why, but I've got a feeling that you're not well. I'm not happy about it. I don't like leaving you alone. Take it—here's a little bunch of violets. All they lack is the scent of violets!"

Without seeing it, Fanny touched the tiny bunch, dewy with water, stiff, still alive and smelling of ditch water like a tiny animal from the hedgerows. She thanked her with a motion of the hand and a tight-lipped smile. The only human being to whom she could have spoken with a hope of being understood sat down at her side. She drew her coat more closely about her and made room for Jane.

"In the café next door, they say that it promises to be a very powerful play."

"Yes, yes—as usual!"

"As usual?"

"But of course, of course: 'A powerful piece of writing', 'a powerful third act', 'an irresistible force drives the tragic characters to their fate'. We've read enough of them, those clichés, you more than I, since you paste up the press cuttings. Farou's 'power' is Farou's flesh and blood. It's his physique, his manner. I've always thought that if Farou had been a skinny little thing with a pince-nez, we would have read something different—'acute perception', or 'many-pointed ironical shafts'. Don't you think so? Tell me!"

"What does Farou think of your point of view? Have you mentioned it to him?"

"It isn't easy to talk to Farou. Have you never noticed that?"

"I have," said Jane.

The curtain rose. On the stage, Mérya and Dorilys were attacking their big scene, the latter pitching high her colourless, nondescript, childish voice, the other using a slightly rasping, velvety contralto. The one intended to keep the lover whom she would not marry, the other fought to possess the same man. On two occasions, isolated and vigorous rounds of applause burst out here and there amongst the half-hundred spectators, like gorse pods in a fire.

"It's good, that!" whispered Jane.

The two actresses redoubled their fictitious coldness and their feigned pride: they sensed already tomorrow's success. Their acting became tinged with that excess of natural behaviour and conviction which brings the theatre down to the level of the basest enthusiasms. Fanny heard Clara Cellerier's voice call out "Bravo!" during a pause which Farou had inserted just to allow someone to shout "Bravo", and the bitter dialogue went on again. This time Fanny listened irreverently.

'Perhaps he really does believe that it would happen like that in real life. He makes me laugh!'

Sheltered from observation, without turning her head, she looked surreptitiously at Jane. Jane was biting her nail and her eyelashes fluttered.

'She is moved. Perhaps she too thinks that it would happen like that. Which day must I choose for her to learn, and I myself to learn, that it does not happen like that?'

Tragic cries assailed her ears. Mérya weakened before a Dorilys who defied her in a Joan of Arc attitude, tense and visionary.

"*You do not know—you no longer know, Madame—what a young girl is like. All the virgin strength, all the untapped innocence I bear within me, the most heinous sin I could commit, the finest deed I could perform—I hurl them all against you, I cast them into the battle for him!*"

In the depth of her soul Fanny was looking at two real, rather dreary, women, self-controlled, careful to avoid raising their voices, to escape a servant's curiosity, to save appearances. . . . She shivered. '*It must come soon. . . . It must come soon. . . .*' A hand passed across the back of her neck and turned up her fur collar, then slipped under her arm and remained in its warm fold, as if asleep.

'Always that hand! What can I do with that hand?

And what if, some day soon, I have to cast off that hand,
forcibly open the fingers which will perhaps clutch at my
arm, at the material of my dress?'

She was more concerned with that hand than with the
end of the act. On her side, Jane watched the coming
and going of the actors with a rigid vigilance, as if she
felt herself guilty of not listening properly. Jean Farou
entered noiselessly and sat in the corner seat, left vacant
by Jane now pressed close against Fanny, and until the
end of the act he lived only for those linked arms, to
curse them, to glower at Fanny, to compel her to release
the refugee arm. With never a word, obstinate, Fanny
fought back, and the curtain fell without her having
yielded.

"Oh bravo!" cried Jane, a second late on the audience's
frenzy.

The curtain was going up and down as at a first night.
Mérya already displayed all the signs of an emotion which
would do her credit on the morrow and, as she bowed,
Dorilys became once more the eternal adolescent on
which the theatrical world could count for another
twenty-five years.

The third and fourth acts, linked by two tableaux,
exhausted Fanny's patience and strength. They absorbed
half the night. Traditional disorder, routine upheavals,
classic technical accidents, delayed the time when
Farou, freed at last, with the frigidity he displayed for
each of his works when the moment came for him to let
it fall, fully ripened, upon the public, could say: "There
is nothing more for me to do here."

Fanny and her two companions joined him on the
stage. Beside him an assistant stage manager was enumer-
ating once more: "The stick of sealing wax forgotten in
Act I, the pocket battery torch which failed to light in

Act II. The door-bell to ring close at hand in Act III;
the coffee did not steam in the cup, also in Act III; less
steel in the moonlight (that's fixed with Julien), and the
type of telephone to be changed. Can you think of anything else, Monsieur Farou?"

"No, no, old man—oh, the lamp-shade in Act II,
not deep enough, the bulb blinds the people in the
stalls."

"Monsieur Silvestre has already noted that."

"I can't think of anything else. Good night, old man!
And thanks!"

His patience was unimpaired, but his eyes wandered
with expressionless activity from left to right and from
right to left over the stage, which had been cleared as if
by magic.

"Where are they?" Fanny was asking. "Where are
they all?"

"Who?"

"Well, Mérya, Chocquart, Dorilys, Marsan?"

"Gone."

"But why? It isn't possible, the curtain is only just
down. I would have liked to . . ."

Farou shrugged his shoulders, strangling himself with
a woollen scarf. "Gone, I tell you. Ouf! They're perfect,
but I can't bear the sight of them—until tomorrow.
Neither can they bear the sight of me. We're sick of each
other, you can understand . . ."

He slipped his arms under the elbows of the two
women and dragged them away.

"It's a great success," said Fanny pensively.

She wished to judge dispassionately and to be just to
Farou for having, as usual, worked alone and loyally.
Since she lacked enthusiasm, she tended to evaluate the
work according to the fruits it bore.

"Yes, it's a great success," she repeated. "I'm certain of it."

They separated to go down a narrow staircase. Farou went ahead, swinging his arms. He cleared the last three steps at a bound and stretched his arms until they cracked. 'What a pity!' sighed Fanny to herself.

She sighed with a confused regret, as she did each time she saw the man who wields the axe, drives a machine, holds the reins and the oars, a close-kept prisoner in Farou's nature. Jean Farou followed the group and cast a shadow with bowed head on the wall.

Once outside, Farou sniffed the rainy air. "Oh, to walk home!" But he flung himself violently into the back of his car, curled himself into a ball and never stirred.

He kept Fanny on his right and Jane on his left. His indifferent hands, for lack of space, lay one on each feminine shoulder. On a tip-up seat, Jean Farou gazed fixedly out on the streets, empty at two o'clock in the morning. At each street lamp, Farou's hand, dangling over Jane's shoulder, appeared out of the shadow, and Fanny could not help watching for this abandoned hand and Jean's obstinate profile each time the light flashed by.

"Half-past two," announced Farou. "Tomorrow . . . a foul day!"

"Oh," protested Jane, "success is certain."

"Doesn't prevent one dying of sleep. Eh, Jean?"

"I'm dying," acquiesced a feeble echo.

The journey seemed long to Fanny and suffering assailed her once more. She feared that the intermingling of her own tension, Jane's agony and Jean's irreconcilable silence would explode into a kind of premature catastrophe before shelter and closed doors had been reached. Farou yawned and stretched out his long legs, let fall two or three trivial remarks and congratulated himself on seeing a veiled moon running between the clouds, heralding fine weather. Untouched by subtler weather signs, he, nevertheless, conjured up by some human reverberation everything which could, there and then, threaten his serene and patriarcal immorality.

11

"IT's funny that they can never type the figures opposite the printed names under 'Authors'. Look, Fanny. Because the typed column is out of alignment, it reads as if we had taken 2,440 francs the night before last, and the Mathurins 22,000."

Jane held out the sheet of box-office returns to Fanny.

"Have you the first week's returns, Jane? Give them to me. Twenty . . . sixteen, seventeen thousand four hundred; eighteen thousand four hundred; twenty thousand three hundred and twenty," Fanny read in a low voice. "That's good, isn't it?"

Jane tossed her head.

"Good? I should say so! It's a fortune, Fanny! And the holidays will soon be here."

"Holidays?"

"Christmas, of course. Three matinées, two midnight performances—and the revival of *No Home* at the Antoine —and the *Grapes* touring in the suburbs! Oh, that Farou! Already he's made it impossible to speak to him," said Jane rather sourly.

"So it's . . . it's really a success?" persisted Fanny. "They're sure now?"

"What a question to ask! Why are you so eager to . . .?"

She noticed that Fanny, whose head was bent over the returns, was no longer reading. She also noticed that she was wearing a new blue frock which slimmed her and made her look as if she were paying a discreet call or going away, and that the sheets of paper were trembling in her hands.

"Well," sighed Fanny, "well, let's get on with it."

She raised a troubled and almost suppliant glance to Jane. The lipstick round her mouth had left exposed a little margin of lip which was a strange mauvish white, and the low December sun darting through the trees in the Champ-de-Mars made her blink.

The same sun bleached Jane's head of young-maize-coloured hair to the palest green, and with a quick movement she slipped out of its rays.

"Let's get on with it," repeated Fanny in dejected tones. "You see . . . My poor Jane . . ."

The beating of her heart and the blood drumming in her ears upset her plan of action.

'What have I said? "My poor Jane"—that was not the thing to say!'

But she was dealing with a rival who would never consent to be over-ridden and who allowed her to utter only a few more words.

"You see, Jane . . . I've found out that you . . . that Farou . . ."

"Wait!" Jane interrupted her. "Wait! Just a moment!"

Sternly, she summoned up her strength. A suspicion of very pale pink rouge, usually invisible, showed on her cheeks, defining their elongated oval shape.

"What are we going to do?" she asked.

Because of the "we", Fanny blushed.

"How do you mean—what are we going to do?"

"Well . . . Is Farou to decide the matter or are we? If you don't mind, I'm going to sit down. I don't feel very certain on my feet."

Once seated, Jane was obliged to raise to Fanny a face

which at first appeared calm enough, being simply devoid
of its usual candour. In order to fight more freely, she
seemed to be keeping nothing but the essentials in her
features, on which could be noted the approach of the
thirties, the changing shape of the mouth under her
rather long nose and the very fine eyes of a jealous
woman.

"Have you spoken to Farou about it?" she continued.

"No, you would have known."

"Not necessarily. I am grateful to you for taking the
initiative."

"The initiative? Were you going to speak to me about
it?"

Jane's hand sweepingly dismissed the suggestion of
such a step.

"No—oh, good heavens, no! I meant, for speaking to
me about it first. So . . . what do we decide?"

Even if assumed, such assurance caught Fanny off her
guard. She knew herself capable of improvising, but only
when moved by anger. For want of anything better, she
smiled.

"It seems to me that what we shall decide is obvious,"
she said.

"Good, I understand. But then, it is *your* decision,
Fanny, and your decision only."

Her imploring grey eyes warned Fanny that she must
not take into account the arrogance of the words, but
sense their underlying motive. Nevertheless, Fanny's
white nostrils dilated and her whole countenance was lit
up by the onset of anger.

"Don't lose your temper, Fanny! Goodness, how careful we must be about what we say! Are you going to
leave Farou out of our—our discussion? Will he remain
in ignorance of today's conversation?"

"Come now, what an idea! That's impossible!"

"Have you thought about it, Fanny?"

"Very carefully."

She was lying. She had merely thought that after she had exclaimed in some fashion or other "I know everything", matters would either be settled or would be fatally disrupted. But all she saw before her was a reasonable young woman, certainly upset, but already arguing, and doubtless preparing to make use of her practical experience and cunning submissiveness.

'She—she's experienced,' thought Fanny. 'She's fought more than one woman over more than one man.'

"I fear," said Jane, shaking her head, "that you've thought less about it than I have."

"Not for as long as you have, probably."

"If you put it that way!"

But Fanny liked neither her pliancy nor her ease of manner. She lowered her head like a horse about to be blinkered and doubled up her chin.

"What is he going to do?" asked Jane in even quieter tones, as if speaking to herself.

Fanny smiled, showing the pale outline of her scarlet lips.

"Are you afraid?"

"Afraid? No! . . . Perhaps I am, after all."

"Afraid of what?"

Sadly, Jane looked into Fanny's eyes.

"But of everything the future may hold, Fanny, of everything which may happen to change our life."

"You can always see him outside," said Fanny in a nasty voice.

"See who? Oh, Farou—I wasn't thinking of Farou."

"That's very ungrateful," said the same voice.

"I owe Farou no gratitude," retorted Jane, raising her eyebrows.

"It's fortunate that you have not claimed him for your own in my presence."

A convulsive cough cut short her breath. Jane made a discouraged gesture, put her elbows on the table and rested her head on her hand. The December sun had already gone from the room and the translucent, aquamarine colour of twilight gave Jane's extraordinary hair a tint of green, revealing a flat, over-broad interval of cheek between nose and tiny ear. A tear streaked the flat cheek and reached the corner of her mouth which absorbed it heedlessly.

"Three and a half years, four—nearly four years," Jane counted to herself.

Aided by a spasm of anger, Fanny threw off her rigid pose.

"I do not require detailed statistics, you know," she shouted.

The tear-stained countenance turned round sharply and Jane surveyed her friend.

"What do you believe, Fanny? Do you really believe that for four years I've been . . . ? That Farou is . . ."

"Don't mince your words! And as for the length of time—we know that has nothing to do with the matter, don't we?"

"Oh, but it has, my dear, where Farou is concerned!"

She raised her shoulders as if she were laughing.

"Fanny, you see before you one of Farou's very ordinary caprices . . . nothing could be more ordinary."

Jane's humility and the bitter distortion of her features revolted Fanny as if they had been low comedy antics.

"That's untrue! Have the decency not to lie! Am I threatening you? Am I complaining? Let us at least finish what we have begun decently—suitably. Yes, suitably."

She was growing hoarse from shouting and, with a wild pleasure, relied on her anger to carry her further. But at the same time, she repeated the word "suitably", attaching to it a moderating virtue. She was met with the shock of seeing Jane, now on her feet, advancing a bold face towards hers.

"What? How do you mean, it's untrue? Then what on earth am I supposed to be? The woman Farou loves, perhaps? You think that I am humbling myself to melt your heart? My poor Fanny! You excused me from giving you statistics, otherwise I'd not have concealed from you the number of weeks which have gone by without Farou condescending to treat me other than as——"

The violent slamming of a door in the flat interrupted her. The pair of them, their hands on their hips, in a pose of acrimonious argument, listened to it.

"It's not him," Jane said at last. "If it were he, we'd have heard the outer door first."

"It makes very little noise since the new draught-excluders were fixed," said Fanny. "In any case, he never comes in here before dinner."

With the sudden cooling off of their anger, they moved away from each other, as if they had tacitly discarded any plan of battle. Fanny went to draw the double curtains across the two windows and light the lamps on both the tables. She sat down, poked the embers and loaded the andirons with logs. She felt the cold of early evening, crystalline and wind-whipped, and shivered despite the central heating and the wood fire.

Now that her spasm of anger had passed, she was less inclined to confront, even "suitably", Jane and the truth, or Jane and untruths. Wisely, and lacking in will-power, she was already saying to herself:

'We were better as we were *before*. Neither of us will reap profit or happiness from what is to come. It would be better if Jane were to remain silent.'

But Jane spoke once more.

"Ah, Fanny, if I could make you understand me. You don't know. You don't know!"

Fanny raised her white forehead with its touching lock of black hair.

"But I'm going to know," she said in dull tones. "I don't see how I can stop you from telling me, now. I beg of you, don't let us be drawn into exchanging the kind of thing—the things which women insist on telling one another about their lovers, their monthly periods and their illnesses—revolting things."

She swallowed her saliva with repugnance. And in contradiction, she added all in one breath:

"Besides, I know enough. And anyway I saw you one day in the bathroom, while he was kissing you, the day you wore an apron and were doing your ironing. . . ."

Shame forbade her to go on. But Jane paid little heed to shame or silence. She pounced upon that memory with a glutton's eagerness for confession and resentment.

"In the bathroom? The day I was doing my ironing? Oh, of course! Ah, that's something we can talk about! Ah, you've certainly hit on a good instance there!"

She began to walk up and down, slapping a flexible paper knife against her palm.

"Yes, yes! Oh, of course—that day! He kissed me as he would have kissed the housemaid, d'you hear what I say? And when I say a housemaid, I'm less than a servant in his eyes, less than all the Asselins and the Irrigoyens in the world! And yet you know what Farou's infatuations are like, come now, Fanny! You've talked to me about them enough, you've demonstrated to me often enough your superior wisdom, your indulgence—your con- donation."

Jane stopped for a moment, shook back her hair and sniffed up tears of irritation. Two meagre little tears shone at the corners of her eyes and she continued to make a smacking sound with the paper knife. The closer Jane came to losing control, the more Fanny returned to an inopportune state of calm resolve, in which she decided that violent emotions did not suit Jane.

'She is made for moderate emotions, ash-blonde sorrow.'

"Really, to hear you, Fanny, one might think you didn't know what Farou was like!"

"He is my husband," Fanny replied.

She had introduced a note of rather pompous simplicity into her retort and this did not please her. It did not produce the reaction on which she had counted, either, for Jane exclaimed:

"Thank God, Fanny!"

"I didn't imagine I should have to thank anyone for that," said Fanny. "Not even you."

For the first time, Jane seemed to be frightened and looked about her distractedly.

"I meant, thank God you were there too, there with him. You feel so terribly lonely with Farou," she con- cluded uncertainly.

She added in the same hasty and hesitating manner:

"Of course, you feel lonely with other men as well. But much more so with Farou. It is perfectly true that I owe Farou no gratitude. But I do owe gratitude to some- one——"

"Charming way of showing it to me!" Fanny burst out.

At that exclamation, Jane subsided, as if it were her turn to be calm and collected.

"I showed it to you, Fanny, as best I could. It was not easy. For the past four years, I've thought so much more about you than about Farou."

Fanny rose, stiff as a poker.

"No," she said. "Not that. Up to now, nothing monstrous has arisen between us; everything, indeed, is extremely commonplace. But I will not stand the sentimental touch. Oh, Jane!"

She hid her face in her hands, and promptly uncovered it so that Jane should not think she was crying.

"It's not a sentimental touch!" protested Jane. "Why should I have thought so much about Farou?"

She beheld on Fanny's features the astonishment which Farou called "the gaping of a pretty fish", and continued impatiently:

"Of course it's not. You assume that anything you don't immediately understand must be a lie. You're so inexperienced, Fanny."

She became milder and stretched a cupped hand towards Fanny's hot face, as though to embrace the smooth, heavy contour of the cheek with her palm.

"So inexperienced . . . so untouched. How very different from me!"

"Yes, yes," interrupted Fanny with an irrelevant thoughtfulness, for childishly she feared the intrusion into the conversation of Quéméré, Meyrowicz and Davidson, and . . .

"You say 'yes, yes', but how can you understand in your present state! Oh, yes, this state of inexperience, this virginal state in which you pass your life. For you, there's Farou, and again Farou, and only Farou, and no other man but Farou. That's all very fine—and then again, I'm not sure that it is very fine—but where I'm concerned, I do not see, I have never at any time seen Farou through your eyes, let us even say with the same feelings as you. It didn't take me very long to distinguish between the two of you, Fanny, and from the moment I did, then . . . Oh, then . . ."

She was growing heated and changing the tone of her voice, as if she had finally reached and almost surmounted the most painful part of their discussion. With her hand she pushed aside, then recouped, all that she wished to express. Sincerity came and went about her like a temptation.

"So, you see, it didn't take long! It didn't take long!"

"But what didn't, after all that?" asked Fanny.

Jane's shoulders twisted under her frock with an affected and provincial awkwardness which Fanny noticed for the first time.

"I find it difficult to say, Fanny. I don't find it difficult to talk to you about Farou. Farou—Farou is a man, an attractive man, a well-known man, who is very gifted. In short, Fanny, I confess that it takes less than that to seduce a girl like me, who has no reason to live by strict standards, to remain chaste and lonely. There is nothing surprising in my having so easily fallen in love, become jealous, unhappy, in fact all that you saw in me. But on the whole, apart from the fact that Farou is Farou, there's nothing particularly remarkable about him as a man. Whereas you, Fanny, you . . ."

She sat down, took her handkerchief and began to weep copiously, easily and discreetly, in a way which seemed to be new and agreeable to her.

She blew her nose and continued quietly:

"You, Fanny, are a much finer person as a woman, than Farou is as a man. Much, much finer."

"Oh," said Fanny with superb haughtiness, "how little you know him!"

Jane turned on her a sharp feminine glance.

"And by the same token," she said, half smiling, "you nearly made me believe that he was incomparable."

"That's it," said Fanny, shaking her head. "It's all my fault now!"

"Yes and no. In a certain way."

No doubt she wished to explain, to expound to Fanny the state of a new and elegant race of serfs, unattached and wandering like winged seeds in the air, with all their adaptability, their anonymous attractiveness, but she gave up in the face of the dark-haired, obstinate female, rooted to her seat, who based her claim on a more ancient code.

"I'm talking about the early days, of course. After that——"

"After that, you became my friend," Fanny answered with a sweetness that boded ill.

"No," retorted Jane definitely. "I was that before. I could not stop being that."

"For so slight a cause?" suggested Fanny.

"Indeed," continued Jane, "there is nothing about me of the siren. Neither am I a mercenary slut, nor an ambitious woman. You can grant me that much. What risk do you run with me? Not much."

"Yes—you would have liked to be the only one to betray me."

Fanny made her point with the same sweetness of tone.

"But your indulgence towards Farou, your damned indulgence, your so-called understanding of Farou, was against me, against us! Your mania for showering him with praise, and curses which were even a hundred times more flattering. Your 'superiority' which consisted in putting Farou at the disposal of all women—did you think that was honourable? I didn't. Ah, no! I didn't! It is a trait which disfigured you, which lowered the opinion I had of you. You," she said as she looked at Fanny with demanding admiration, "you were a finer version of myself."

She moved away, raised the window curtain for an instant and promptly let it fall back, as if to hide what she had seen in the grey night. She returned to place her hand on Fanny's shoulder and shook it slightly.

"And just now you asked me if I were afraid? But I'm shaking, I'm ice cold with fear, Fanny! You, you're just thinking of getting rid of me, you think that petty physical matters of love are crimes if I'm mixed up in them, you think you're going to tear Farou away from me—as if he hadn't attended to that himself long, long ago! You think you're going to cleanse your house and perhaps fumigate my room. It's unbelievable that anyone should make such a fuss about love! A man isn't so important: he isn't eternal! A man is . . . a man is only a man! Do you really believe that you meet a man, on his own, just like that, alone, free, quite ready to devote his life to you. A man is never alone, Fanny—and indeed it's rather horrible that he should always have a woman, another mistress, a mother, a maid, a secretary, a relation, a female of some sort. If you only knew the various types of women I've found round a lover! It's horrible—the word is not too strong!"

She clutched her forearms so tightly with both hands that her finger-tips turned white. Abruptly she poured herself out a glass of water which she raised to her lips first, then on second thoughts she held out the glass to Fanny.

"I beg your pardon. I'm dying of thirst."

"Me too," said Fanny.

They drank in silence, as courteous to each other as wild animals keeping truce beside a stream. Emotion had affected each in a different way: Jane had red patches upon her cheek-bones and Fanny was pale, with smutty circles under her eyes, and her mouth, devoid of lipstick, was a negroid mauve. After she had drunk, Fanny emitted a lengthy sigh of fatigue and Jane again made as if to cup the curved cheek in her hand, without touching it.

"Poor Fanny, what a lot of trouble I give you! Would you like to . . .?"

She dared go no further.

Fanny said shortly, "No thanks," and concentrated on trying to recall the exact words of a scolding Jane had given Farou long ago.

'She said to him, "You'd much better give her your hand" or "hold her hand", I can't remember exactly. She also said to him that day they thought I had fainted, "Don't knock her feet against the door", or something like that, and "Is that the way to carry a woman?" '

"You taught me the desire to serve," said Jane softly.

Fanny could not control her agitation, rose to her feet and began to walk round in small circles, as she did when she was merry, with the supple and agile movements of a plump creature.

"No," she said. "No, I can't stand it! Since everything is spoilt, you must change your way of speaking, you must stop appealing to our emotions and exploiting that bond, that past, that——"

A door opened behind her.

"A-a-a-ah!" yawned a great joyous voice. "All these women! All these women! What a lot of women I've got in my house!"

He had returned dishevelled and pleased with himself. His handsome golden eyes, languishing and inscrutable, announced that he had just come from a brief bout of pleasure or from a long spell of work. Easy money for a few months and renewed success adorned him with a youthful air, in no sense unseasonable but foreign to his nature, and he wore it like a spotted bow tie.

"I've just met Pierre Wolff," he exclaimed. "I must be looking remarkably fit, because he threatened me with arterio-sclerosis, the shaking palsy, and——"

He became aware that neither Fanny nor Jane had stirred when he entered the room. He examined the two faces, saw that they had both changed completely from what they had been that morning, and asked in masterful tones:

"What's the matter?"

"Farou . . ." Fanny began.

"Fanny, I assure you!" begged Jane.

"What's the matter?" Farou repeated intolerantly in louder tones. "Women's quarrels? Rows with the servants?"

Fanny looked at Jane and gave a little laugh. The whole of Jane's body gave fleeting signs of a kind of mimed politeness, as if to tell her, 'I'm leaving you free to speak'. To which Fanny replied with a nod, 'I'll take charge of everything.'

"Farou," Fanny continued, "Jane and I have just had a serious talk. You see that we are quite calm. We intend to remain so."

She spoke with lips over which the mauve pallor had entirely encroached, and pronounced her words with care. Farou just had time to notice the pallor of his wife's mouth, and the pervasive glaze over her too big, too beautiful eyes which no longer expressed anything. He must have thought that she was going to faint, for he put out an arm towards her, but she made her meaning clear.

"Jane is your mistress. I am your wife. We cannot decide anything completely without you."

Farou, who had sat down, rose slowly to his feet. His

brows were knit majestically and, for a moment, the two women were afraid only because they thought him handsome. Both waited for they knew not what thunderbolt to fall.

"Which of you brought it up?" said Farou at last.

"I, of course," declared Fanny, offended.

His glance rested upon her without anger, but with already calculated mistrust.

"Had you known it long?"

She lied from a kind of bravado.

"Oh, a very long time."

"And you hid it so well? Congratulations!"

She considered this a vulgar counter-offensive and shrugged her shoulders.

"But," Farou continued, "if you really have been hiding it so long, what astonishes me—yes, what astonishes me is—why didn't you continue to do so?"

Thrown off her balance for a moment, she recovered herself and cried:

"Do you think one can keep a thing like that to oneself —that one can be silent for ever?"

"I'm certain of it," said Farou.

She made a gesture of appeal to Jane as she stammered, "Well, that's the limit—that's the limit——"

"You especially," added Farou.

"Accustomed to it, no doubt?"

Until then Farou had watched Fanny's trembling hand, but he now saw that her eyes were filled with tears, and gained confidence.

"Accustomed to it—if you like to put it that way. Whatever I may have done, have I ever abated one iota of my affection for you during the past twelve years?"

At these words, Jane stepped smoothly and softly forward into the light, and Farou started.

"I am well aware, Jane, how particularly painful this scene must be for you. But I beg you to remember that every word you utter will make it more painful still."

"But I did not wish to speak," said Jane.

"What's more," Farou continued, "I am ready to assume the entire responsibility."

He was interrupted by a sharp exclamation from Fanny.

"What do you mean? Responsibility? What responsibility? Who asks you to be responsible? That's not the point, Farou! Say what you want, do something, pay some attention to us, but not in that way! Quick, Farou, quick!"

She was horror-struck that at such a time he should have been able to control himself, and was already accusing him of respecting the age-old convention of a man caught between two women. How was it that Farou had not yet stormed, dispatched human justice and delicacy to the devil, as well as any feelings Jane and she might have, and carried off in his arms the object, if only temporary, of his burning choice. 'How slow he is! God, how slow he is! Violence—but a passionate violence for one of us, never mind which! Despair—but a passionate despair! Are we all so old that he should remain so calm, that he hasn't even sworn at us?'

"We are not lunatics," said Farou. "I am only a man, but a man who has decided to preserve a sense of proportion in a situation in which so many men and women lose theirs. If, in regard to Jane, I have been——"

"I don't enter into the argument," Jane intervened. "I'm not aware that I've made any claims? I only enter into the argument if Fanny wishes me to go away, which is quite natural."

He acquiesced with a grave nod. Behind his male

strength, bold outline, beneath his mane of hair, Fanny sought for a manly decision, a trace of the emotion which Jane's words had roused within herself.

"Fanny knows perfectly well," said Farou.

He corrected himself and addressed his wife.

"You know very well, Fanny, that you are my dear Fanny. And for my part, I have always been fortunate in your affection for me, whatever our ups and downs, for more than ten years. Those same ten years should be an assurance to me that you will be able to spare the woman who deserves to be spared. I thank you in anticipation."

"The woman who deserves to be spared" received the end of the speech and Fanny's stupor without so much as a flicker of the eyelids. She even pursed her lips and indicated a whistle of ironic admiration. Since Farou's entrance, she seemed to have lost the power of feeling deeply or of being astonished, and her eyes narrowed as she watched Fanny and Farou's movements.

"What does that mean? Farou, what does that mean?" murmured Fanny in consternation.

She turned again to Farou just in time to see him stifle a yawn of nervous exhaustion.

'The longing to be far away from here is oozing out of his very pores!' thought Fanny, white with fury. 'He's going away! He's going to find an excuse for going away. Is that all he's got to say? Is that the way to finish, or begin, a new chapter in one's life?'

"Farou!" she called in sorrowful anger.

"Why, yes, my Fanny, I'm here. I'm listening to you. Would you like us to have a talk alone?"

"Farou!"

She rejected the gentleness, the thoughtfulness with which he treated her like a delirious invalid. She would willingly have dug a knife into Farou so as to see something spontaneous, irrepressible, gush out of him, blood, curses, suffering.

Farou took the risk of putting a hand on her head, and bent over her as he tilted back her forehead. In the depth of the large yellow eyes, Fanny saw the desire to convince her by sensual means, but beyond that again, it seemed to her there lay a spirit of precaution, hidden, wary, and rather cowardly. Her madness retreated to the depths of her soul and, bending her neck, she caused the heavy hand to glide over her hair.

"Listen, Farou! I'm in no state to talk to you. You came in too soon, do you understand? That's it! You came in too soon."

"All the better," said Farou with great dignity. "My place is here. Let's get all this settled."

Fanny looked thoughtfully at him, her courage fled. In her turn, she wanted to speak to him in tones of deplorable kindliness.

"No, Farou, let it go. All Jane and I have to do is to finish our conversation and come to some practical arrangement tonight, without fail. Nothing shall pass between Jane and myself to make us raise our voices— isn't that so, Jane?"

"Of course," said Jane. She was still standing in the same place, slightly behind Fanny, her eyes watchful.

"Good," acquiesced Farou. "Good. I see nothing against it. I hope that you have no objection to my staying next door, in the study? I can be sure that nothing which concerns the three of us will give rise to public scandal? Not even to servants' gossip? Can I be absolutely certain?"

He took advantage of his unfinished question to make slowly towards the door, walking backwards, impressing each woman in turn with his dominating yellow glance.

"Yes, yes, yes," Fanny repeated each time. She nodded impatient assent and, in the end, the black cable of her hair uncoiled itself. She hastily gathered it together with both hands.

Farou's attention never wavered from the two unhappy faces and from the thick flowing hair which was being twisted by white arms. Through his eyes passed an offer of peace, unseen by Fanny, but such that Jane advanced aggressively towards Farou.

"Yes, you can be certain. But let us talk to each other alone."

Farou obeyed with a strained little smile. Jane followed him to the door, shut it and came back to Fanny who had just finished putting up her hair again.

"And that's that," said Jane, drily.

"Yes," sighed Fanny, completely overcome. "That's that!" She let her arms fall to her side.

"Have a rest, Fanny. There's no hurry."

Fanny went back to her armchair beside the hearth and huddled over the fire. The entrance of the maid, passing through the room, obliged Jane to sit down and run through Farou's mail and the documents of the Authors' Society, which she pretended to sort out. The maid came back through the drawing-room again, carrying Farou's dinner jacket and shirt.

"He's going out," said Fanny in a low voice.

"Yes," said Jane, "it's the performance for the dressmakers at the Gymnase. Are you going to it?"

Fanny did not reply. Hunched up in her chair, her breasts against her knees, she stared at the fire. Jane, barely leaning against the back of her chair, appeared to be waiting for her relief from sentry duty. She made some entries in a notebook, seemed to be making mental calculations, and looked at her wrist-watch.

At about seven o'clock Jean Farou came in. Fanny answered his "Good evening, Mamie," automatically and did not move. But such an outrageous and tell-tale scent emanated from Jean Farou that both women raised their heads simultaneously.

"Is it you who are smelling like that?" asked Fanny.

"Like what, Mamie?"

It was to Jane that the boy dedicated his dark-circled lids, his shining, feverish, swollen mouth and his youth darkened by its fall, directing them to her like a mulish insult. His laugh was harsh and he brought the vulgar scent, the scent of another woman which at long last announced his deliverance, for Jane to inhale.

"Go and change," Fanny ordered him. "You make us sick."

He went out, proud of being understood and blamed.

"Would you believe it?" said Fanny. "How nasty a little boy growing into a man can be! For two pins he'd bring her here. So proud to have a mistress all for himself!"

"For himself and against me," said Jane.

"That's true."

They felt themselves strictly alone and spoke without restraint.

"He does his best. He does himself an injury so as not to love you any more."

"Oh, love me! Perhaps enough to wish to injure me. Perhaps he has already done so. I'm not asking you any questions, Fanny," Jane added quickly. "If you are willing, while we are undisturbed, let us speak briefly and to the point. Let's say that I leave tomorrow——"

"No, no," Fanny interrupted her, "later, after dinner. Can't you hear that they're already laying the table."

Jane gave her friend a long look.

"You wish me to dine here?"

"But of course. Come now!" said Fanny at the end of
her tether. "Don't let's complicate matters."

"Very well. You're right. I'm going to put some things
away in my room. If you need me . . ."

When she returned she found Fanny in the same place
beside the dying fire. She whispered to her: "Fanny,
dinner!" And Fanny, after a summary toilet, made her
way to the dining-room, in which lingered, although
less strong, the scent Jean Farou had brought back with
him. With exceptional courtesy, Farou stood waiting for
his wife to be seated.

Fanny noticed that he had shaved closely, had combed
his hair and discreetly dusted his face with ochre
powder. His dinner-jacket fitted tightly over the hips
and his head was held high above well controlled
shoulders. 'Who the devil is he after tonight?' she asked
herself. 'Perhaps it's me?'

Once seated at the table, she felt completely exhausted,
cowardly and ravenous. She ate a large meal, to the surprise of Farou, who watched her as he talked to his son.
Jane also talked to Jean, who, not without impertinence,
paused with marked surprise before replying. As Farou
ceremoniously tilted the bottle of champagne towards his
wife, she laughed at him.

"I don't know why, but tonight you look like a young
tragic actor playing a comedy part!"

And she began to laugh easily as do the convalescent
or the very weary. She was thinking: 'And my sorrow—
what becomes of my sorrow in all this? When shall I
have time to nurse it? Today there has been a place for
reason, anger, for everything except that. They'll finish
by taking it away from me.'

Farou's departure from the house was subtly contrived,

and carried out with agility while talking, lighting a cigarette and putting on an overcoat. Fanny thought he was in the hall and Jane thought he was in the bathroom when he was already crossing the street. Facing Jane alone again and slightly tipsy with the dry wine, Fanny shook her head.

"That's what I call, by way of an exit, the charwoman style."

"What?" asked Jane, taken aback.

"Haven't you ever noticed that one never knows the exact moment of a charwoman's departure? She vanishes like a sylph. It's because she always takes away with her a small memento, a slice of veal for her husband, what's left of the coffee in a bottle, the scrapings from the sugar-bowl."

She laughed again. But in the salon in which she took refuge, someone had already revived the fire and spread over the arm of a favourite armchair the big vicuna wrap, and sorrow in its most selfish form sent a lump to Fanny's throat. The idea of being left alone, the threat of being alone so soon, dispersed the transient warmth which she owed to her copious meal. 'One is so lonely with Farou.' She sat down, placed the wrap round her legs and closed her eyelids over two tears.

"Am I in your way?" asked Jane in a low voice.

"No, no," said Fanny without opening her eyes.

"Would you rather we had our talk now? Yes? I can get Delvaille by 'phone tomorrow morning early. She'll really be delighted to get her job back."

"Who is Delvaille? What job?"

Fanny was taking the comb and pins from her hair and laid her head back on its streamers of black damp seaweed.

"Why, Farou's former secretary, don't you remember her?"

"Not Delvaille, Jane! No, no, not Delvaille!"

"What has she done to you?"

Beneath her unbound hair and her oriental pallor, Fanny opened eyes that were as moist, wild and gentle as those of a drowned woman. She gathered herself together with difficulty to drive away the image of a former Delvaille, short, plump, active and pregnant. Delvaille at work. And Jane? And Jane? Jane not there, Jane vanished.

"Nothing," she confessed. "But there are really more urgent matters than sending for Delvaille. Can't Farou's scribbles wait? Farou's scribbles can go to the devil!"

"I don't mind them going to the devil, but not if they land on you! Think it over."

"Exactly. I'll take time to think it over."

She fell back on her pillow of hair. When Jean Farou, dressed to go out, came in suddenly, she moaned.

"Are you still ill, Mamie? You're ill much too often. Why not see a doctor? I only came to say good night to you."

He kissed her finger-tips and she noticed that he had changed the way of doing his hair. On his wrist he wore a thin gold chain and in his shirt a jewelled stud, which she had not seen before. The two women read, as if writ large, these hall-marks stamped on him by a woman.

"Luckily I leave you in good hands. Good night, Jane."

He went out with a light-hearted, cruel expression.

"Now he's pleased," said Jane. "He's made his exit, if I mistake me not, with a 'poisoned shaft'."

"Poor kid!" said Fanny absent-mindedly.

"Oh, really!" Jane took her up. "You've better things to do than to pity *them*."

Her use of the plural made Fanny thoughtful. The

crackling of the fire and the regular pecking of a needle made her drowsy.

"What are you sewing?" she asked, suddenly waking up.

"I'm restitching my thick gloves," said Jane. "This leather is so tough, you can't wear them out and they're very useful for travelling."

"Ah, yes."

Fanny shuddered at the word "travelling". She visualised the cold, the whistling wind, arid white platforms, and saw the hotel bedroom with its naked bulb hanging from the ceiling. She was not the kind of woman to exile herself voluntarily; she could imagine no other form of loneliness but to be ignored, nor any other form of decision but to wait.

The houseboy came through the room bearing mineral water, oranges and two glasses for the bedside tables.

'Oranges and two glasses?' Fanny said to herself. 'It's true, Farou will be coming home.'

She was apprehensive of the night hours, of the beds and the twin bodies, of Farou, and perhaps of his amorous strategy which was not without its dangers.

'I know him,' thought Fanny humbly. 'He'll be more brilliant than he was this afternoon. Oh, this afternoon...'

"Jane," she exclaimed, "couldn't you tell me...?"

The seamstress waited, needle in the air. She had not concealed her real face behind the mask of a young-girl-on-the-verge-of-thirty, and she smiled with heavy sad hollows in her cheeks.

"I can't see what there can be I couldn't tell you now, Fanny."

"Then tell me if you don't agree with me that, today, Farou showed himself to be incredibly . . . That he was . . ."

She could bear it no longer, rose, and allowed herself the relief of exclaiming: "I thought that he was beneath contempt, but also beyond contempt! Why was he beyond contempt?"

"And how then would you have liked him to be?" retorted Jane pointblank. "Did you expect him to be witty? Or that he would beat you? Or throw me out of the window? A man in such circumstances! But not one man in a hundred ever gets away with it to his advantage, if not to his credit!" She shook her head.

"It's much too difficult for them," she concluded without further comment and as if keeping the most illuminating part of her experience to herself.

"Why?" asked Fanny feebly.

Jane bit off her thread.

"Because . . . it's like that. They're shy, you know," she said, still using the same unflattering plural. "And besides, they're so made that when involved in what we call a row, or an argument, they always see at once the chance of getting rid of us for ever."

Fanny did not reply. She was harking back to long past, passionate days, when she wept and screamed with jealousy before a silent, detached Farou, who had retired to one of the mountain fastnesses from which the male antagonist watches his dearest possession, his superfluous encumbrance, whirling and falling through space. She walked from one window to the other to ease the stiffness which numbed the whole of her body. She stopped in front of Jane and looked at her searchingly.

"Have you a definite purpose in speaking ill of Farou to me in this way?"

"A purpose? No."

"Or at least a motive? A plan? An intention, an idea? Come now!"

Her hands moulded her loose, deep-rose gown over her hips and she shook a smoky cloud of hair over Jane.

"Do you mistrust me?" asked Jane, her lips quivering.

"No, I don't mistrust you yet! But why do you speak ill of Farou?"

Jane narrowed her eyes, focussed on the study door, but she clung to an original grievance, as if it would have taken longer to explain the man than to accuse him.

"It's out of resentment," she affirmed, meeting Fanny's glance steadily.

'Out of resentment,' Fanny repeated to herself, 'just as in the case of Quémérè, of Davidson—and so?"

She could not understand that Jane could treat Big Farou like a mere Meyrowicz, or that Jane could use only the word "resentment" to describe the ingratitude, the sardonic harshness, with which the female of every race repays the male from whom she has escaped, though not unscathed.

"Out of resentment," Jane insisted, "out of resentment. It is so. You don't even understand, do you? It's because you are Fanny. You're much too clean-minded for all that sort of thing, dear . . . dear Fanny."

She had at last dared to capture the hanging hand and was pressing it against her cheek. The hand protested agonisedly, slithered and grew limp so as to escape, and Jane took up her needle again.

'It is here,' thought Fanny in front of the black window pane. 'Now the hour has come when I must decide if I shall force open that hand I was expecting. That hand closed over my wrist, resting in the hollow of my own, cupped under my elbow, that hand on my arm, that hand clasping my own during our walks in holiday time. I was certain I would have to deal with that hand which brings me the vicuna wrap, pulls up the collar of my coat, tends my hair, the hand that met my own under the damp sheets during little Farou's illness. It is the same hand, dyed with duplicating ink, which stained Farou's fingers purple and denounced him to me.'

"It's freezingly cold between the two windows, Fanny."

'But,' Fanny continued as she returned obediently to the fireplace, 'where shall I find the scales, and if I did, what right have I to weigh what I owe to that hand against what it has taken from me?'

She fell into a long reverie which at times was close to slumber. Whenever she opened her eyes again or turned them away from the fire, her glance wandered round the room, strewn with tall lampstands and large shades.

On one of the tables, Jane placed documents and files. "Farou's scribblings."

"Is everything there important?" asked Fanny.

The round head of hair, shining with clear gold and silver, and the young, tired face turned quickly towards her.

"Not in the slightest. But he insists on everything being kept. It's a mania. That's his look out. You may be sure that I'm leaving everything in apple-pie order."

The warm silence closed in again, attacked by unobtrusive noises from outside and protected by the low, even chatter of the fire. Towards eleven o'clock Jane rose, taking the documents and files into the study.

'Tomorrow,' mused Fanny, 'tomorrow, if she goes away, I shall be like this, alone beside the fire, like a woman who has come to the end of the greater part of love. Perhaps Farou will take it into his head to keep me company—that would be the worst of all. For he would batter the walls from the window to the fireplace, break down the panels, or fall asleep with his head on his shoulder in that armchair. Or else he would work next door, seeking Jane at every moment and cursing the pair of us. At the end of the week, he would have replaced her. But I, I shall not so easily replace her. As for him, he is bound to find another of the kind he prefers, a passing favourite. He will once again recover his innocence, his loneliness and his profession. But what about me? Where am I to find someone once again to keep me company? Two of us are not too many to be alone with Farou—to stand up to Farou.'

She raised herself from her armchair and looked for a book or a pastime; the green table was folded and no longer awaited the litter of cards.

'Before the days of Jane, there was at my side a fair-haired little boy, very sweet, who played cards with me. For a long time he was twelve years old. I've lost that little boy. He was charming and the sound of his voice, his shyness, his frail health, used to bring something feminine into our home, where henceforth there will be only Farou. I am no longer young enough, or rich enough, or brave enough to remain alone with Farou—nor far from Farou.'

She tried to form a clear picture of Farou, stripped of its conjugal glamour. But the effort wearied her as if she had been straining upward to follow the flight of one of those silent birds which fly in great circles round a nest on which they never alight. She considered a few steadfast couples and tried to assess how large a share of a man women can get for themselves.

'Pooh! The only certain thing they possess is to be able to talk about their man, complain about him, boast about him and wait for him. But everything they flaunt could just as well be done without the presence and existence of a man!'

She was aware that she was denying the remains of a

pure religion, whose faithful lived solely by waiting for their god and by the childish ritual of their cult, and she turned again to the help which could spring only from an alliance, even if it were uncertain and slightly disloyal, from a feminine alliance, constantly broken by the man and constantly re-established at the man's expense. . . . 'Where is Jane?'

"Jane!"

Jane came at once. Although her face was grey with fatigue, she was ready to sit up all night, to answer each call, to work with scrupulous care.

"Jane, don't you want to go to bed?"

"Not before you do."

"Are you waiting for Farou?"

"Not without you."

She sat down on the other side of the hearth, facing Fanny, and thoughtfully poked the fire. She was listening attentively to the after-midnight sounds, and suddenly kept still because a car slowed down as it passed along the street.

'When I flay Jane, I find Farou again in the first drop of blood,' thought Fanny. 'Tomorrow, the day after to-morrow, later on, the same will happen to me if she happens to strike me.'

The heavy front door was heard to close downstairs, then the gate of the lift on the landing. Jane's eyes questioned Fanny nervously and she rose.

"Where are you going? It's only Farou come home," said Fanny with exaggerated calm.

But Jane, her face sheet-white, confessed her fear by stammering.

"A scene . . . So painful . . ."

"A scene? With Farou? My dear," said Fanny, who was resuming the advantage of her seniority, "it's out of the question. Why have a scene with Farou? We have mixed up Farou far too much in everything that concerns us. It's my fault," she added with a slight effort.

They listened to the slow fumbling of a key. Footsteps in the hall made towards the study, stopped, and returned thoughtfully towards the salon. Then their sound changed, they became light, and faded away.

"He's going away," Fanny said very softly.

"He saw the light under the door. Perhaps you ought to go to him?" Jane suggested.

Fanny shrugged her shoulders. With the fingers of both hands she lifted the weight of her hair from her neck to cool it, put her feet closer to the fire, and peeled an orange.

"There's no hurry," she said at last. "We've plenty of time. Is it very late?"

"No, no—barely half-past twelve," Jane assured her. "It's so cosy here," she said with secret anguish. "Tomorrow, I'll——"

"Hush, Jane! Who's asking you to think of tomorrow? Tomorrow is a day like any other. It is cosy here. . . ."

After that, they exchanged only a few desultory, commonplace words. As one pretended to read and the other to sew, their sole desire was to refrain from speech, and allow those inner reserves, which the man had not dared to affront, to subside and sink to rest, relying on silence to foster their frail, new-born security.